CONFESSIONS

Rabee Jaber

CONFESSIONS

Translated from the Arabic
by Kareem James Abu-Zeid

A NEW DIRECTIONS PAPERBOOK ORIGINAL

First published as New Directions Paperbook 1329 in 2016
Manufactured in the United States of America
New Directions Books are printed on acid-free paper
Design by Erik Rieselbach

Library of Congress Cataloging-in-Publication Data
Names: Jåabir, Rabåi°, author. | Abu-Zeid, Kareem James, translator.
Title: Confessions / Rabee Jaber ; translated from the Arabic by Kareem James
    Abu-Zeid.
Other titles: I°tiråafåat. English
Description: New York : New Directions, 2016.
Identifiers: LCCN 2015045958 | ISBN 9780811220675 (alk. paper)
Subjects: LCSH: Lebanon—History—Civil War, 1975–1990—Fiction. |
Orphans—Lebanon—Fiction.
Classification: LCC PJ7840.A289 I8513 2016 | DDC 892.7/37—dc23
LC record available at http://lccn.loc.gov/2015045958

10 9 8 7 6 5 4 3 2 1

New Directions Books are published for James Laughlin
by New Directions Publishing Corporation
80 Eighth Avenue, New York 10011

For Renée and Marwa

MY FATHER used to kidnap people and kill them. My brother says he saw my father transform, during the war, from someone he knew into someone he didn't know. That's my big brother—I never knew my little brother. I know his picture, I know his face, he looks more like me than my big brother—that is, in photos he used to look more like me—and I call him my little brother, as all of us used to call him—in our heads, even if we didn't actually mention him in our conversations, his pictures still filled the house—what was I saying? I call him my little brother even though he isn't my little brother, and I call him "little" because he stayed that way, because he never grew up, because they killed him when he was a boy.

How many times did I see my sisters sitting silently in the living room (the safe room, our refuge in times of shelling) as if they were at a funeral, side-by-side on the long sofa with the green velvet cover, gazing at the enlarged picture of him on the wall, a black ribbon hanging over the corner of it. How many times did I see my big sister turn, in tears, and watch me enter carrying a sandwich—I ate sandwiches all the time: the shelling died down at sunset and my mother would rush into the kitchen, warning me not to follow her,

1

but I always did. I ate those mortadella and pickle sandwiches as fast as she could make them. I can recall my sister now as if all these years had not passed—they passed and they didn't—I remember her turning to look at me from beneath her long lashes, her black hair framing her white face, and I remember how she'd raise her eyes and look at the picture. . . . I can recall the moisture on her lashes, I haven't forgotten that. I didn't know at the time—how could I?—that my sisters weren't able to look at my face without feeling their hearts break, split in two. . . . To this moment I haven't forgotten my sister's face, how it transformed, the love and hate, the confusion and fear and anger. I didn't understand how her expressions could suddenly appear like that, only to melt away and be replaced by others. How could her face be so transformed in the blink of an eye? Clouds don't race that quickly across the sky. . . . What was she feeling when she looked at me and then at the picture? When we passed each other in the corridor, between the living room and the kitchen, my big brother often pushed me in the chest to move me out of his way and I would turn toward him and see the strange expression on his face as he looked back at me: as if the sight of my face was repulsive to him. He'd bare his teeth like a wolf, I didn't know why. . . . So much time has passed and yet, even now, I still don't know how to tell my story. All of this is hard. All these years have gone by and I'm still at a loss, still unable to speak, as if the words themselves were clogging my throat: I can feel them rising from my belly, from my heart. And as I finally speak, it feels like the mud is leaving. But it's not mud.

This memory is one of my oldest from the house in Achrafieh—it might be from the very last days of the Two-Year War, but I'm not sure of the exact date. But I know it's from that period—that much I know—from the last part of the Two-Year War, not from '75, yes, from '76, I'm sure of that, and not the beginning of '76, because at the beginning of '76 I was bedridden, feverish, caught between life and death—I didn't open my mouth back then, didn't speak a word. I was saved, a new life was written for me. What I remember from that time—the time of my illness—is dark and strange and fluid. I'll talk about it later: all of my memories from that first period are jumbled, and I don't trust them, I don't know if they're real or imagined, if they've become intertwined with dreams, if they're stories I later heard from my sisters and my big brother and my mother (my father didn't speak much). My oldest memory— the oldest one that I know belongs to me, a real memory and not someone else's invention, not my own invention either—is from the Achrafieh house: my father burning clothes and notebooks in our backyard. I can still see the fire and the wood, the stove made of large stones. I remember the fire was outside the stove, on the ground, where my mother used to set her large washing pot (the electricity went out a lot back then, and my mother and sisters would do the laundry by hand under the peach tree), and I remember my father, his darkened face—he didn't look like my father— and how his face clouded over while he pulled things—I didn't know what they were—out of a deep sackcloth and threw them onto the fire, as the tongues of flame leapt to lick his eyelids and the hair on his head. He was inching around the fire, slowly, and I stayed inside by the kitchen table, not moving a muscle, holding my breath while gazing through the open door. Even now I remember my fear. I didn't know what was happening.

But I have another memory from that period as well, a memory I love and always enjoy calling to mind: all of us were in the family room and the shelling had stopped days earlier, maybe weeks earlier, I can't be more specific, but the feeling of safety was almost complete, as if there were no threats of the ceasefire being broken at any moment, even though no one trusted the "ceasefires." No, it actually felt like peacetime, but the war wasn't over—the Two-Year War hadn't ended yet. We were sitting there as if the war weren't happening, as if the war had never even taken place. All of us were in the family room, gathered around the wooden fold-up table as my mother poured hot *kishk* porridge into bowls. My father cut the bread and passed it around—I remember his big hands and the hair on his fingers, and my brother taking the sliced loaf from him, uncovering it, and placing a piece between him and my little sister—she always sat next to him, on his right. One of my sisters laughed as she watched. My little sister split the piece of bread in two because she didn't eat much. We were scared she was becoming anemic: she never ate anything—she liked drinking milk but didn't like eating—all this is part of the same memory: When I recall us sitting together on that distant morning, eating warm *kishk* and watching the steam rise from our bowls, which were quickly becoming empty, I remember countless details about my sisters, brother, and parents. I remember, for example, the knife in my big sister's hand as she peeled onions, and how she cut each onion into four pieces to pass around. I remember the basket filled with onions, and how the peels were piling up. Years later, I started having unsettling dreams: I saw that very same scene, but with different faces. I saw a big stove in the middle of the room, and slices of white onion on top of the stove, slices that were turning black over the flame. I saw a loaf of bread being toasted beside the pieces of onion. The entire scene was changing before my eyes: it wasn't the Achrafieh house anymore, it was a different house. And I saw faces, at once strange and familiar. Who were they? What did the memory mean? All of this—back in that earliest period of my memories— used to torture me. Torture me? That word doesn't mean what I want it to mean. I was confused and didn't know why. I didn't know why the confusion wouldn't dissipate, why I took such an interest in those incomprehensible dreams.

There's another memory from that period, this one's not mixed up with any other memories, this one's flawless, and dear to me as well: My mother was in the kitchen making sweets for us. It might have been a holiday. She was kneading dough, preparing trays of *maamoul* cookies, and I remember the dates on the table, my big sister crushing pistachios—but more than anything else I remember the flour on my mother's dress, the smell of lard and rose water, and the warmth of the place—the stove filled the room with heat. My mother was half-asleep when she looked at me, she almost seemed to be dozing off, as if she were making us *maamoul* in her sleep, as if she'd been drugged, as if she were moving in a dream and mixing the pistachios with—was it lard or butter?—I don't know. . . . The memory is distant, and sometimes I think it's my oldest memory, not that other one, the one with my father burning things. I don't know. Maybe it isn't very important. (I often tried— and soon you'll find out why this is so important—to determine the age of those first memories, arranging them systematically so that I could understand them, so that I could perhaps find my way back to the beginning. . . . But this is difficult, extremely difficult, and then there's the fact that memories can be deceiving: I used to sometimes remember the peach tree in bloom behind the house, not far from the stove, but sometimes that same tree would be black and completely leafless in my memory, so dry that if a single flame from the fire my father had started touched it, the whole tree would've burned to ash in an instant. Memories can be deceiving, and in my case they deceived me twice. They deceived me twice, for I'm not myself.)

One more memory and then I'll continue: My father was carrying me on his shoulders and plunging into a river. I held onto his head so I wouldn't fall, and my big brother laughed as he helped my sisters across. My mother waited for us on the other side of the river, and she was laughing too. (My father had carried her across first. He carried her on his back, and I still haven't forgotten how she laughed and how my sisters laughed as he plunged into the green water and disappeared for a moment under the shadows of the green trees before reappearing on the other side. I think it was the Abraham River, I think we were spending the day there. We often used to go up to the Mar Charbel Monastery and the Abraham River. We'd take a picnic basket and spend the whole day up there, not returning to Achrafieh until sunset.) I remember the river rising almost to my face before receding, while my father stepped between the stones and the water drenched his legs and pants, which he'd folded up above the knee, and I remember the smell, the smell of tobacco and his sweaty shirt—his smell. I remember one of my sisters was calling me, and I turned around to look at her, still riding on my father's shoulders as he held onto my feet—his hands were huge, and he was laughing. I looked at my sister: I saw her standing by the car, a blue Peugeot (a Peugeot 504, which was new—at the time you only saw the old white Peugeot 404s on the streets of Beirut). I saw her standing by the car, the hood nestled between the broom shrubs and the thistle—my father had parked it like that to scare my mother, he had taken his time applying the brakes. The doors of the car were open, so was the trunk. My sister stood by herself, a radio in one hand and a bag in the other. The large red radio had a broken dial, and she had to move the tuning needle with her finger whenever she wanted to change the station. I remember the clear laughter and the running river—these sounds are still in my mind. The sunlight poured onto the river, and the beads of light glistened on the beads of water. I helped my brother gather wood while my father started a small fire, and my mother kept an eye on my sisters as they stabbed skewers through the meat.

I can't doubt these memories: they're part of who I am. All of this is me. But . . . Listen: during the war, in that first period from my memories, the world was unclear to me—maybe it wasn't because of the war, but rather my age, how young I was: I was little, I was often scared. Yes, I remember that, I can always remember my fear. My big brother was afraid too, but he feared for my mother. I learned to love him by watching him love my mother. He used to take care of her as if she were his own daughter. You wouldn't believe how he took care of her, how he looked after her back then. Did he really take care of her as if she were his daughter? No, but he cared for her as if she were his mother and he were hers alone, as if he were her only son, as if he were all she had in this world. He used to berate all of us whenever he saw her tired or lost in sadness. If she wore herself out doing chores around the house, he'd yell at my sisters, even though all of them—with the exception of young Liliane—used to help her.

My father kept silent as he listened to my brother, who would calm down if he noticed my father could hear him—when my father was present, my brother seemed broken, defeated. He never pushed me in the presence of my father. He's nine years older than me. Once he pushed me down the stairs: I stumbled, lost my balance, and hit my head against the wall. A drop of blood oozed from my temple. He was on the verge of tears as he picked me up and made me swear on my mother that I wouldn't tell anyone. I promised I wouldn't say a word, and I asked him why he'd pushed me. We'd been playing, and I had no idea what had happened. Something had changed in him for no apparent reason, as if he'd remembered something, as if something had suddenly crossed his mind—and in the blink of an eye, he'd turned on me.

In the beginning, things—all things—were incomprehensible. I remember my mother at church, during Mass, placing her warm, trembling hand on my head. She was crying, but I didn't know why. My eyes were glued to the man standing at the altar, who was holding a large heavy censer from some chains, a censer the color of gold. He was swinging it in front of him, in front of his broad chest covered in fine dark robes.... The hymns mingled with the incense, filling the vast space of the church, while my mother's hand—heavy, hot, trembling—remained on my head, as if she were probing my skull. Why was her hand shaking like that? It felt like a small animal was weeping on top of my head. What was wrong with her? People were turning around, showing me their faces (neighbors I knew, women I'd seen, whose names I'd learned from my sisters, and also some women I didn't know, women who weren't from this neighborhood—I saw a lot of strange faces at Mass). Perhaps they were staring at me, but I wasn't sure—they could've been staring at my mother, or maybe their eyes were fixed on my clean and ironed clothes, I don't know. They never wore those unfathomable masks while looking at my sisters, and when my big brother used to come to church with us I never saw their faces change like that when they looked at *him*. Was I imagining things? I went back home feeling weak. It was as if something had left me, as if the strength had left my body under those gazes. I was young—I didn't think like that back then, but now, when I remember the young boy I was, that's how I remember him. Now I know him better than he used to know himself.

I remember him in the living room, by himself, raising his eyes to the picture hanging on the wall. He looked at his little brother and saw the reflection on the glass. The photo was enlarged, in a black wooden frame, with a black ribbon hanging in the upper corner. He didn't climb onto the sofa, didn't lift his hand, didn't touch the frame of the picture. His little sister often touched the frame of the picture, but he didn't know why. Was she touching the frame, or trying to touch the smiling face beneath the glass? His older sister would wipe the glass with a wet cloth. She'd wipe it slowly, and I often saw tears in her eyes as she did so. I can only ever remember her wiping it with tears in her eyes, even though that's not logical, even though I know it's not true — I know she wiped the dust off her little brother's picture countless times without tearing up. One changes with the passing of time, life becomes routine, and as she wiped the glass she no longer thought about what she was doing and continued cleaning, wiping dust from the sofa's wooden headrest and from the small table where her father kept his stone ashtray.

Does one change with the passing of time? Ilya — my big brother — used to tell me my father changed from one person to another in a single night and day. "In a single night and day" — I haven't forgotten my brother's expression — it's remained etched in my memory, and I recalled it at different hours of my life: I often remembered this expression because I thought that I too — like Ilya and my father — had changed in a single night and day. Ilya didn't say my father had turned from a man into a beast — others said that. Ilya later told me a lot of horrifying things. Ilya had changed, too, when he heard those things. People we knew who had relatives in our neighborhood, people who spent time in the Sioufi district, had seen my father in Jisr al-Basha. They said they were passing by that part of town and when they saw my father they couldn't believe it was him. But it *was* him. He was forcing people out of their cars and beating them. He was shooting them and throwing them off the bridge.

Ilya used to tell me these things, his voice unwavering, unshaken. That was a long time ago, but when he told me, it felt like no time had passed: was it true that all those years had passed? We were in the Rizq Hospital — it was quiet that night. My father was in the operating room, and my brother was speaking. I didn't know if I'd ever see my father alive again. Meanwhile, my brother was telling me about that "beast" on the bridge in Jisr al-Basha and in the Tel al-Zaatar and Karantina districts. My sisters had gone and would be back in an hour (the doctor said the operation would take a long time), and Ilya started to speak. I don't know what came over him. I don't know what I was thinking when I heard his words, but I knew the place had changed: as he spoke, the chairs in the waiting room vanished, the door that opened out onto the balcony vanished, and the ancient trees disappeared as well—everything vanished: the statue at the end of the corridor, the white walls, the life I had known. I no longer knew where I was. I was supposed to be in the waiting room, it was supposed to be nighttime, and the sick were supposed to be sleeping in identical beds inside identical rooms. This balcony was supposed to look out over tall trees (cypresses? evergreens?) in the hospital's central courtyard, over there in Achrafieh, that part of town that I knew like the back of my hand. We were supposed to be there, my brother and I, and in a little while my sisters were supposed to return: we were supposed to be waiting for my father, waiting for him to come out of intensive care. Isn't that right? Was he still under the knife? Was he still in the hands of the surgeon who my sister knew, whose wife she knew, whose apartment she'd visited in the Berty Building—was he still in the hands of the most skilled surgeon not only in Achrafieh, not only in East Beirut, not only in the whole city, but in all of Lebanon? This must be the waiting room—I know the smell of antiseptics—and I'm with my brother waiting for my father to come out of the difficult operation: they're opening his head now, they're in there opening up his head beneath the bright lamps and removing the tumor with delicate instruments. The tumor was pressing onto his ocular nerves, and he was in danger of going blind—the doctor had said—if we don't remove the tumor it will keep growing and growing until . . . Until what? Until it becomes larger than his brain?

This isn't your time, Ilya, this isn't the time for your memories. Ilya was talking about how my father had, in the span of a single night, turned into someone he did not know. I didn't understand why he was telling me this now. I always asked him about it, but he had never said anything. . . . Why was he talking now? Why was he opening his mouth at this precise hour? Why was the dam breaking now and the mud pouring through? I was sinking in that mud.

No one ever spoke in front of me. I always wanted to hear about my little brother, but no one said anything. I waited a long time, a very long time. And they waited till the most difficult hour before they finally told me: I call him my little brother even though he isn't my little brother. I call him "little" because he stayed that way, because he never grew up, because they killed him while he was still a boy.

No one ever answered my questions. I remember when my sister Najwa broke her leg during the Hundred Days War, after the Two-Year War. In the Hundred Days War, there was so much shelling in Achrafieh that not a single windowpane remained intact in the whole neighborhood. One day, when our house was still shaking from the bombing, my sister disobeyed my mother (my father wasn't home) and left the sanctuary: she left the living room—a natural, centrally positioned safe room whose only window was blocked off with sandbags. She left the sanctuary and went to the kitchen. She was hungry. She said she'd go grab some bread and a package of cheese, but she was lying. She wanted to climb up into the small pantry above the kitchen to get something sweet: a jar of jellied peaches. In times of danger, she always asked for sweets. She fell off the ladder as she was climbing into the pantry and broke her leg.

Later, I stayed with her while she recovered. She was bedridden and in pain. She would send me to get something for her and I'd come back as quickly as I could. That was when she began feeling my face with her fingers, feeling all over my face as if I were made of glass, and saying that she loved me, saying that she loved me a lot. I was young and didn't understand. I still don't understand. She'd touch my face and say, "My darling Maroun, I love you so much, Maroun." And I'd reply, "I love you too, Najwa, my sister." Often she'd start to cry. Something deep inside me, something dark and secret and untouchable told me that all of this had something to do with my dead brother—but I couldn't understand what or why. I was young, and when you're young you don't think about such things. You welcome the intense emotion, the passionate touches, you embrace the body that's embracing you, and you don't ask yourself too many questions. That love is enough for you, that sweet flood of emotion, that warmth suffices. You ask for nothing more when it's raining outside, and once the shelling dies down you can hear the wind blowing through the peach tree. Why would you ask for more? I remember the little boy I was, scrawling with a pencil on the cast on the broken leg, and I remember that little boy's sister, Najwa, with her dimples, Najwa who used to bite into tomatoes as if they were apples, who used to pull that little boy toward her, playing with him and running the white ivory comb through his hair.

"You're my darling, Maroun." Her words remain, like honey. When bitterness struck, did her words become bitter too? I want to tell you my story. But it's hard. You have no idea how hard all this is for me.

Ilya said my father punched himself on the head: "He hit his head with his own hand." Ilya said my father was holding the telephone receiver with his left hand, and then he lifted his right hand

and punched himself on the head. His head reeled from that blow, but he rushed out of the house, still in his slippers—he hadn't put on his shoes.

It's important I tell you the story in an orderly fashion, but I keep getting accosted, distracted. I feel powerless, I feel . . . The images flood in and I'm powerless to stop them. But I'll try.

In order to tell you my story, I need to start with my little brother. They kidnapped and killed him. He hadn't reached his tenth birthday when they kidnapped and killed him, when they dumped his body, the clothes all torn, on the road that climbs from the "Museum"—the demarcation line area—to the Hôtel-Dieu Hospital in Achrafieh. One of the Phalangists, a relative of my uncle, recognized the tiny bloody corpse and called my father—but the news would've come in even without that man: my father had put up pictures of my little brother at all the hospitals and police stations, he put them up at the offices of the Phalange and the National Liberal Party, he put them up at the Civil Defense Offices and the League building, he gave them to the newspapers, he even passed them out in stores and in the Flippers arcades. Ilya took the pictures and made the rounds to all the shops. And they enlarged the picture as well, and Ilya went off with my father and our cousins: there wasn't a single wall in all of Achrafieh that didn't have that picture, not a single wall in the entire area around the demarcation line. They put it up everywhere, and added, beneath the picture, his name and our address and telephone number. Some people called and demanded a ransom—it later became clear that these people had nothing to do with the kidnapping, that they were simply trying to profit from the situation. . . . But these details are meaningless, only the outcome matters. They called my father from the Phalange office, and then they called him from the Hôtel-Dieu Hospital and told him to come and identify his son. Ilya saw my father punch his head, jump up, and leave the house in his slippers. From that moment on, he was no longer himself—that's what Ilya said.

My father didn't go alone, Ilya stayed with him, and some of our neighbors went with him too, including Doctor Philippe Broadwell—who would later treat me for bullet wounds. Ilya used to love that doctor because he looked after my mother, and had it not been for Broadwell's medicines, my mother would have died long ago. On several occasions they caught her just as she was trying to jump off the roof. One night, while they were napping, she escaped from the house. They found her smashing her head against the wall by the *ful* and hummus restaurant at the corner. The road stretched out in front of the restaurant. The kids used to play soccer around there, and sometimes they'd kick the ball in the air and it would land in the fenced-off garden in front of the mayor of Achrafieh's house. The mayor's wife would scream while my little brother laughed. She told my mother he was a devil. Everyone in the neighborhood used to call him "the little devil." They told my father that. And they told my grandfather about it too, whenever he came to our house. They called him "the little devil." He used to break windows with that soccer ball, but they all loved him. Light-skinned, blond, quick, and full of laughter. They kidnapped him and killed him, his clothes torn up and his body bloodied, on the road that climbed from the Museum to the Hôtel-Dieu. He wasn't alone. There were seven young children, seven tiny stiff corpses laid out in the back of a van.

Ilya saw my father standing in the long white corridor with the small body in his arms. He was walking unevenly. His shoulder kept bumping into the wall. Ilya said my father wasn't crying. He said he couldn't forget the movement of my father's body: how he leaned on one side and kept crashing into the wall, and how he'd immediately straighten up again—like a crumbling pillar: toppling, then returning to its place. Ilya said my father had no face at that moment, that he looked at him and didn't see a face. "He wasn't crying." Ilya repeated those words several times as we sat in the waiting room at the Rizq Hospital. We were waiting for my father to come out of the operating room, and Ilya kept talking and talking and talking. And all the while I thought I was in Hell.

Ilya said my father held the small corpse in his arms as he left the Hôtel-Dieu. People from the hospital and some of our neighbors tried to stop him, but no one could hold him back. He took my little brother's corpse and walked to the apartment of one of our relatives from the Estefan family. That apartment was near the Hôtel-Dieu, and it was empty. My father had the key with him — the owners were in France — and he'd been going to the apartment every two or three days to keep out thieves and squatters who'd been displaced by the war.

"He had no face," Ilya said — he only saw my father's face when he turned around and told Ilya to go home, to return to the house ahead of him. The building guard opened the gate for my father. The rattling of the many keys resounded through the empty house, and the screams of neighbors rose up, then suddenly died off. Where had those voices come from? Ilya only saw my father's face when he spoke: he told him to go to the house, there was a small container of medicine on the dresser by the bed, a green container, and put three pills in a cup of water: "Not one pill, and not two. Put three pills in the cup for your mother and don't tell her what's happened, I won't be long."

Ilya wouldn't go. Ibn Broadwell (the doctor) spoke with my father and asked him what he wanted, but Ilya didn't hear what the doctor said, nor did he hear what my father replied. The doctor left, and so did the neighbors, but Ilya stayed with my father in the Estefan family's apartment.

Ilya stayed with my father and the corpse. Inside the house, he saw things and didn't see them. In the Rizq Hospital, after all those years, Ilya remembered everything as if he were remembering a dream. It wasn't a dream. As he spoke, I felt the breath, the soul, leave my chest and not return. I saw Ilya there with my father and our dead brother, seeing things and not seeing them, in an empty apartment in a half-deserted building. I saw the building with its shattered windows, which looked out over the demarcation line, through to the other side and its snipers. I saw the nylon stretched over the window frames. I saw the small body with its torn clothes on the dining room table. I saw Ilya. He was alone. He was with my father, but he was alone. My father said something, he spoke as if the words had come from another world, from another life: he wanted to wash my brother, he wanted to wash the blood from the boy before his mother saw him. Ilya said the blood had dried in his hair, and they washed him with soap and warm water. The guard came to help too. And the guard's wife. But my father wouldn't let anyone touch my brother's body. He washed the boy himself with the warm water. Ilya said the body was like wood, like a piece of wood, like a statue—not a boy. He was nine years old, just over four feet tall, and weighed fifty-three pounds.

After the funeral, my mother was bedridden. I don't know anything from that time, these are all Ilya's memories. My mother stayed in bed, drugged, and my father began to disappear from the house, and when he returned carrying a weapon the neighbors stayed out of his way. He smelled different. And his face looked different. His beard grew, as did the hair on his head. Around that time, rumors began to spread about massacres at Tel al-Zaatar and Karantina.

Wait a second: don't think I'm going to tell you a story you've already heard before. All of us have lived in this country, all of us have lived through horrible stories, or at least heard horrible stories.

What I'm about to tell you is unlike anything you've ever known. I know that each person thinks their life is unique and bears no resemblance to any other. People are like that, I know, and I know every life is precious, and that no two lives are the same — I know all that, but let me tell you: My life really *is* different. I won't tell you stories you've heard before. Eighteen years have gone by since the end of the Civil War, and now we're on the brink of a new war, soon we'll be killing each other again. The papers are saying it, the people are saying it, but I don't think they're right. I don't believe it because we fought each other for fifteen years, and we need a break. Maybe we'll start fighting again in forty or fifty years — that's what Ilya says. "I wouldn't advise anyone to start a family in this country," that's what Ilya says.

I won't tell you what my father did in Karantina, and I won't tell you what my brother did after that. My father committed atrocities, my brother too. My brother less than my father, my brother was forced into it, or at least he says he was — but my father never said anything, he never spoke about that time, and when he did finally speak, he only told me one story (the story that concerns me), and never told me any others. He hated talking, my father. Everything I know about Karantina I learned from others. Now, as I tell you all this, I can see the buildings in front of me (before they were torn down), and I can see the willows lining the wet road. There was a chill in the air. They were separating the families, ordering the men to gather beneath the stairs, ordering the women and children to go out into the street. They said they were going to take the men to be inspected, but they sprayed them with bullets instead. I won't tell you what happened after that. I want to tell you the story that concerns me.

My father didn't take part in many battles, but he kidnapped and killed I don't know how many people — sometimes a hundred or even two or three hundred people would disappear in a single day. Right here, in Beirut. "Black Saturday" was one of those days. But there were many others. I told you I spent part of the Two-Year War sick, hovering between life and death. And I told you my first memories are confused, all jumbled together. A long time passed, after the fever and the loss of all that blood, and for a long time I could only move slowly, sluggishly—my body lacked strength. I used to hold onto the table, the sofa, or the edge of the bed as I moved among the rooms of the house, not knowing where I was.

How accurate are my memories? Remembering is difficult, you can't imagine how difficult this is for me. I remember myself and I don't. It's like I'm remembering a life someone else has lived. Strange, this feeling. And at the same time not strange at all. Listen: In the first days of winter, when the cold sets in and the rains begin to fall, I always feel a pain in my chest. Every year, every single year. Often the pain in my chest is so sharp that I have to gasp for air. What do these small things reveal?

When I started college in West Beirut—after the end of the war in 1990—I thought I was entering dangerous territory. I was careful about what I said, and I noticed that I, like my father, didn't like to talk much. I didn't realize this until after I started college. I began thinking about my father a lot back then, and tried to understand him—but how can you understand someone who never stops building walls around himself? I have pictures and countless memories of my father. Sometimes these memories suffocate me. But it's Ilya's memories of him that suffocate me even more—and also my sisters' memories of him, and especially memories from early on in the war, especially those memories.

He used to disappear from the house for days and nights on end. There wasn't a single person in the entire Sioufi district who didn't know what he was up to—half the makeshift roadblocks at the crossings were of his doing. He had certain companions who never left his side, even for a moment. His reputation kept growing, until they came to know his name over there, on the other side of the demarcation line—that's what Ilya said. Was he exaggerating? If he wasn't exaggerating, if all of that was true, if . . . Listen: All of this is exhausting, I'll keep it as short as I can.

He kidnapped families and killed them. He kidnapped them on al-Sham Road, he kidnapped them at al-Burj Square, he kidnapped them behind the Lazariyyah Complex, and at the Museum, and at Bechara al-Khoury. He kidnapped them at Sodeco Square, at the al-Sayyad circle, by the Monteverde district, he kidnapped them on the bridge in Jisr al-Basha. . . . He went all over the place, everywhere, kidnapping and killing, kidnapping and killing. Years later, Ilya stopped me behind the Collège des Frères in Gemmayze and showed me some bullet holes in one of the walls. "We used to gun them down right here," he said.

How many years have passed since the Two-Year War? Thirty-two? Thirty-three? As I speak now, I feel as if I'm more than one person: there's someone inside me who wants to talk and talk and talk, and there's someone else inside me who wants me to shut up, to shut up forever, to never open my mouth again.

My father used to kidnap people and kill them. In one of the narrow streets by al-Burj Square, in one of those alleys not far from the square, he stopped a white car and asked the passengers for their papers. Two men were up front, and a woman was in the back with some children. The driver was shaking—he was terrified. How had he come here? Had he entered the alley by mistake? Lost his way? Had the car brought him here of its own accord? He was terrified. And so was the passenger in the front seat. Was the woman in the back his wife? And the children . . . three or four children, who were they?

My father wasn't alone. He was the leader of the group. Something happened — maybe nothing happened, maybe that's how it always went down — and they opened fire on the car. The car was stopped: the road had been blocked off with barrels and with my father's car. Where could that family go? They opened fire on the car. It was raining. A light drizzle had been falling all that day, and my father and the men with him were wearing raincoats. Maybe the driver had lost his way because of the rain, because the car had a broken wiper, because he was afraid of deserted spaces. There were stores and offices in the square, and restaurants and parking lots, buildings and theaters. But this place, this alley near the square, was deserted. This was by the demarcation line. The frightened man had lost his way, the car came to a roadblock, and men in raincoats emerged from the shadows and opened fire on the people in the car.

The woman in the back held onto the children as the broken glass rained down on her. She held onto the children while the bullets spilled blood from her body. One of the armed men opened the door to the backseat to fire from close range. A little boy jumped out. He was four or five years old, blond, and fair-skinned. He was crying convulsively (warm blood was streaming from his body), he looked like he'd just woken up: that look was on his face, the look of a boy who'd been woken unwillingly from sleep.

He was wearing a white wool sweater. Blood seeped from its collar, and the stain kept on growing until it covered his whole chest. My father saw him and drew nearer to look at him. He motioned his friend away (the machine gun was still warm) and picked up the boy, who had fallen over. He wrapped the boy in a blanket and took him away.

The doctor said the boy would die from the bleeding. But still they gave him bag after bag of blood. And they removed the bullets and shards of glass from his body. The doctor said the boy would die, and asked my father where he'd found him—the doctor knew my father—we found him on the street, my father said. The doctor said he'd die. But the boy didn't die. His wounds became infected; his fever rose. They thought there was no hope for him. But he didn't die. When he was finally better, when he opened his eyes to find himself lying on a bed in a house and not in a hospital, he didn't open his mouth. He opened his eyes and looked at the faces that were looking at him. He heard words coming from a distance, but didn't understand what he was seeing and hearing. Did they ask him what his name was then? Maybe no one asked him. He was four or five years old, and had come back from death. He was cured, and my father named him Maroun.

    — *He named him after you?*

    No. I'm Maroun. I'm the boy they kidnapped.

I'M MAROUN. I'm the boy they kidnapped. Didn't I tell you I wasn't myself? Didn't I tell you my whole life has been strange, didn't I tell you that I've always struggled with my memory, that my memory ran circles around me and twice deceived me? Dreams brought back images, and those memories perplexed me, it was like walking through a forest at night: what you remember overpowers you, it beats you down into the earth again and again, walking all over you, coming and going, paying you no heed, and leaving you lying on the ground with no way of grasping what you've remembered (where did this dark memory come from?) or how you remembered it. You might recall, for example, what I told you about us sitting down for a meal, how we ate warm *kishk* porridge around the table, how my father passed the bread to my big brother. . . . Do you remember that? When I went to college and lived in a dorm, when I moved away from our house in Achrafieh, I began having incomprehensible dreams. I'd had them before, or ones like them, but this time it was different — I felt that something was changing inside me. . . . How can I describe it? It's better to tell you things in order, better to go back and tell you everything from the beginning.

They shot me in 1976, on the demarcation line that split Beirut in two, and my father picked me up and took me to his home. Rabee, if you ever write about my life one day, I want you to begin with that sentence: *They shot me in 1976, on the demarcation line that split Beirut in two, and my father picked me up and took me to his home.* But he isn't my father. I know that now. And at the same time, he really *is* my father. A light rain fell all day, and on that day I was given a new life. I lost one life and gained another. . . . Gained? And the other people they killed in the car? Do you think I don't care? Do you think I didn't look for my family when I found out? Don't judge me until you've heard my story. I'm only at the beginning.

My father, the one who'd been kidnapping people and killing them ever since his little boy had been murdered, his bloody corpse with its tattered clothes dumped on the road between the Museum and the Hôtel-Dieu (they dumped all the tiny corpses on the side of the road, in a vacant lot—there's a building there now, with restaurants on the ground floor, where the lot used to be), my father, the one who carried me, bloody, from the demarcation line, was not my father. But he *was* my father too. Before that, I had (is "had" the right word?) a different life and a different father, a different mother and different siblings. I didn't have just one life. I had a name that was different from the name I've come to have. I had a name other than my own. My father carried me to Achrafieh, and when I opened my eyes, when he realized I was going to live, he named me after the little boy whose picture was hanging on the wall of the living room, a black ribbon in its corner. He named me after the son who'd been taken from him. He named me Maroun.

The woman who helped the mayor of Achrafieh make a fake identity card for me is still alive. Her name is Evelyn Azar. I'll tell you later how I went and visited her in her house in the Ramil district, and I'll tell you what she said. They gave me my dead brother's name, and the ID stated that I was the son of Felix and Victorine, and that I was born on September 29, 1971, which makes me a Libra. (This might seem silly, but my whole life I've continued to believe that I'm a Libra and I've remained interested in that sign, even though I'm not a Libra—my passion for horoscopes comes from my sisters, Najwa in particular.) When I was young I asked my sisters why I had the same name as my brother, how that was possible. They said my mother vowed to Saint Maroun that she would name two sons Maroun.

This is the order of my sisters: Julia is the oldest; then comes Mariana, who we call Mary; then Najwa; and Liliane is the youngest. I'm closest to Najwa, even though she now lives the farthest away, and even though she generally doesn't see things the way I do. All of them are here now except Najwa, who's in France. Julia has four children: Eli, Philippe, Georgette, and May. May was born in Canada, after they left Lebanon for Toronto, but they've returned now. They might leave again, I don't know. Mary has three children: Carol, Lisa, and little Tony. Liliane has a daughter, Nathalie. Najwa isn't married, but she has a boyfriend in Paris—before that she lived with a different boyfriend, but she lives alone now and hasn't married yet.

In the house in Achrafieh, Mary, who's a year younger than Julia, acted like the oldest. Julia tended to be lazy and stayed out of the way. Mary was the cook in our family, after our mother. My mother taught all the girls to cook, but Mary had a knack for it. My father only drank coffee that was made by either my mother or Mary. Whenever Julia made him a coffee, he used to say . . . No, not my father, my father didn't say that—Ilya was the one who used to say that this isn't coffee, it's black water—yes, Ilya used to say that. My father would drink Mary's coffee while he smoked his cigarettes on the balcony in the morning. He'd go into the bathroom when he was done, and a little while later he'd leave the house. When he got back, he'd climb up to the thatched shelter on the roof where he raised canaries. He spent half the day between the balcony and the roof, moving the cages from the balcony to the roof, or from the roof to the balcony, depending on the weather. That was after 1985. He didn't raise birds before then.

My father was a different man before '85. How many times had he changed? Did he change? My mother died in '85. Her weak heart killed her. Over the years father took her to countless doctors, there wasn't a single hospital he didn't take her to. Ilya wanted her to travel to Europe to receive treatment, but she refused to leave the country. The doctors here told her there was no cure: her heart muscle was weak, too weak to withstand an operation or any other kind of treatment. The muscle shrank and atrophied. It was like having the heart of a small child in an adult's body. I can't recall my mother without seeing all the pill containers on top of the dresser by the bed, and in the dresser's upper drawer, and in the lower drawer as well: countless pills, along with folded-up pieces of paper that were removed from the containers so Najwa could read about the side effects while Julia asked about this or that substance and Mary stood in the doorway with a wet towel between her hands, her sleeves folded up past her elbows, a drop of sweat running down her forehead. All I can remember is my mother lying in bed or on the couch, swallowing pills and repeating "O Virgin Mother," with my sisters gathered around her.

Before her health deteriorated, she'd been quite active: she cooked and cleaned and swept the floors, and always prodded my father to take us to Mount Lebanon. Her favorite trip, the trip dearest to her heart, was to the Mar Charbel monastery. She only conceived a boy (Ilya) once she'd made a vow to Saint Charbel. She loved the saint, and a framed picture of him stood on top of her nightstand. I remember her wiping off the icon of the Virgin Mary with some oil, lighting the candle, and turning her head in my direction as I watched her, afraid she'd burn her fingers on the match (when I remember her now, she always seems drugged, half-asleep), and she raised her pale hand, with long fingers and a slender wrist, and it seemed like her fingers were too heavy for her, as if her wrist couldn't bear the weight of those bones. . . . I haven't forgotten how she used to lift her hand to summon me, I haven't forgotten how I'd rush to kneel beside her on the sheepskin rug, how she'd take me in her arms until I disappeared in her warm body, how she'd say my name over and over again. She'd hold my head and smell my hair and say words I couldn't make out because one of my ears was pressed beneath her arm and the other ear was crushed against her chest—I didn't know what she was saying, but I told myself she was praying for the Lord to protect me.

Ilya always worried about her, and she always worried about me. I studied at the Nazareth School before moving to a different school, but both were close to the demarcation line. The Nazareth School was open when things were calm, but it would close whenever the clashes and shelling started up again. But often the school would be open and we'd be in class when the shelling started. They'd gather us together on the ground floor because the windows there were covered with sandbags. When that happened, the electricity would go out—the reserve generator usually broke down too—and the only lights the teachers had were matches and lighters. Later on they got some gas lanterns for the ground floor, as well as some battery-powered fluorescent lamps. I remember one of the first times, I'm not sure what year exactly: I remember the scared faces, and I remember the girls in their blue school uniforms, and I remember one of those faces looking straight at me: her name was Hilda, though her name's not important, but if you want to write down a name, write down Hilda Sufayr. She used to ride the bus to school with me, she was from the neighborhood. We grew up together, at some point life took us in different directions, and then we met again. I loved her and wanted to marry her . . . Did I really want to marry her? I think so. I'll tell you later about what happened and what her father said to me.

We met again when I was about to finish high school, when I was preparing for the college entrance exams. She'd transferred from that high school to a different one years earlier, and whenever I crossed paths with her—in front of the gas station, or at the intersection by the park, or in front of the *ful* (fava beans) restaurant that became, years later, a bakery for *manakish* sandwiches—we'd exchange a few polite words without thinking too much about it, without remembering anything from the old days. . . . But when I started going out with her afterward, when we went to the movies, out to eat, or to the park (the one in Sioufi) or to Kaslik, when we started growing closer, those memories emerged from my depths and I began to talk about things, asking her if she remembered them, too. She remembered some things and didn't remember others. In the shelter, when I saw her looking at me in the school's shelter—yes, she remembered that. She laughed and said she'd been looking at everyone, not just at me. But that's not important—the important thing is that she remembered. There were other things I'd tell her that she didn't remember. They weren't important. They weren't things that were directly related to her or to me—no, that's not what I mean. I'd ask her if she remembered such and such a teacher, for example, the math teacher who always used to come to school wearing sandals, who had such and such a car, and she wouldn't remember. I found that strange. I'd tell her a bit more about the person and she'd remember—and sometimes she'd remember even if I didn't tell her anything else. Maybe she didn't remember right away, right then and there, but later she'd tell me: Remember that teacher you talked about? I remember him, it came back to me two days ago. Or she'd say: Remember that field you told me about, the field with all the banana trees just past the school where they used to toss out the old chairs? It suddenly came back to me this morning, just like that, while I was packing my bag.

Are you wondering what all this has to do with the story I was telling? I'm trying to make a point about memory. Memories are misleading. When I remember things from long ago, am I remembering what actually happened? And you, do you think *your* memories are real? You remember things from long ago, but they're not here anymore, right? For example, you remember a room in your family's house, a room where you often used to stretch out on the sofa and look out the open window at a patch of sky, or at the balcony of the building across the way, or at a tree—to what extent is that memory real? Maybe the house isn't there anymore, maybe the whole street's changed. Isn't that right? Buildings change, trees die, and all that. . . . Isn't that right? Memories are misleading. The trees were there before, but where are they now? I think about these things a lot. And I wonder: Can one go back to those places?

One day, my mother saw me playing soccer in front of the house and started to cry. Then she said I wasn't allowed to play soccer anymore. I didn't understand it. Ilya took me aside and said he used to love soccer too, but he'd stopped since mother didn't want him to play. And he asked me to do the same, for her sake. I wanted to know why but he wouldn't tell me. Later on, Julia said something vague about my little brother. I didn't understand exactly what she was saying—whenever anyone talked about my dead brother, things became vague: they'd trail off mid-sentence and never finish what they were saying. All my sisters were like that. Even Najwa avoided talking about him. But I put the story together from their few scattered hints: Like me, my dead brother used to love soccer, and he used to leave the house a lot to go play. And one of those times they kidnapped him.

I stopped playing soccer in front of the house—I wouldn't play anywhere in the neighborhood, not even in the park. For a while we used to play soccer in the abandoned train station by the park. But Mary saw me once—or rather, she said she saw me from a distance and recognized my blond hair and my shirt. She said she recognized my hair, but I wasn't convinced. Mary was like that: she'd say the craziest things and then laugh at me when I believed them. But that time I didn't believe her. I found out how she knew I'd been playing: my socks—the red sand had stained my socks. I went to great lengths to keep it from them. I wouldn't come home till I'd washed my face and hands—and even my hair—at a sink in the station. And whenever Julia saw me enter the house with messed-up clothes and a red face, I'd say we'd been running, or that we'd been playing hide-and-seek, but that we hadn't been on the field. You're not a child anymore, she'd reply, so why are you playing hide-and-seek? Are you lying to me? Do you want to upset your mother? Do you . . . She'd raise her voice just a bit, just loud enough for me to worry that mother would hear us from her room. I'd swear to her that I hadn't been playing soccer. I'd swear by Jesus Christ the Savior and by our Mother Mary—and I felt no fear.

Although I swore like that, I wasn't afraid of going to hell—what was hell? I wasn't afraid of Satan's fires, and why should I burn?—because I played soccer with my friends? I wasn't afraid of those small lies (I lied for my mother's sake, so she wouldn't worry), but I was afraid of other things. And when the stories I heard started to multiply, I became even more afraid.

They'd tell stories in school. There was a playground where none of us ever played because it was exposed to sniper fire (a row of buildings shielded the school on the other side, the side closest to West Beirut). There were some kids playing in that playground one day — it wasn't big enough for soccer, it was quite small, and there was an old olive tree in one corner where the concrete gave way to dirt — yes, the kids were playing there (this happened before I was at that school) and one of them fell to the ground. What were they playing? They were playing tag: one of the boys would run after the others to tag them, and when he got you — it was important that he didn't tear your shirt — then you'd be "it," and it was your turn to chase the others. Or maybe they were jumping rope. Does it matter what they were playing? The playground was full of children eating sandwiches that they brought from home, drinking soda, scrambling around, and laughing and telling stories and jokes (it was the 10 a.m. recess). There was a terrible noise, then a burst of laughter, and in the middle of all that a boy fell to the ground. No one had pushed him, but he fell.

They'd tell stories at school, and they'd point out the black spot on the concrete, in the fenced-off playground that we weren't allowed to enter (there was a gate with a lock and chains). If a ball flew over the tall wire fence and landed over there — in the forbidden playground — it was gone forever. No one dared climb the fence to get the ball: we were afraid of sniper fire, and even more afraid of being punished. We were afraid that the principal or one of the administrators would see us.

As I remember this now, I can picture deflated balls on the concrete, behind the fence. I'm not sure if this is a real memory — am I imagining things? And I can see a ball that wasn't deflated, a ball that was still round because it hadn't been hit by sniper fire. But no one climbed the fence to get the ball. We knew the sniper was waiting. We knew he'd left the ball as a trap.

The most horrific things we heard were stories of kidnappings. Shelling was easier than kidnapping. Shelling was clear and simple: the bombs would fall, and they wounded or killed people. We used to collect the cold shrapnel off the street (Mitri, the son of George Tayyan, put them in glass jars and sold them to a man who had a store in the Tabaris district). We weren't scared when we gathered up shrapnel. Shelling was something we knew: this is a 106 shell, we used to say, and this is a 105. But kidnapping: What did they do to the ones they kidnapped? I knew things no one else knew—I, the boy who used to get dressed each morning in the living room beneath the picture of my dead brother on the wall, I knew things. I used to sleep in the living room with Liliane and Najwa. We'd spread out on the sofas and go to sleep. Other times, depending on how things were, the whole family would sleep in the living room.

I knew things, but not completely. What happened, for example, to the ones who were kidnapped but whose corpses were never found? Where were they? Who was holding them? And where exactly were they holding them? What were they doing with them? All of that was black, dark—the stuff of my nightmares.

I was a growing boy, and whenever I outgrew any of my clothes, Julia or Mary brought me some more from the closet: I'd never seen those clothes before. There were many closets. (There was a closet in my mother's room, a closet in the family room, which we called the "winter room," and one in the sitting room, though we rarely ever sat in it because it was open and exposed to the shelling. There was also a closet by the stairs that led to the roof, and another one in Julia's room, which wasn't really a closet, but a bunch of boxes that Ilya had painted white and stacked on top of one another— Mary had sewn a curtain for it, and stitched green grape leaves in the corner of the curtain.) Clothes and socks had been stuffed into the depths of the closets, along with lavender and dried leaves from other fragrant plants, which kept the moths away. I remember how someone's hand would slowly take the clothes out and give them a good shake. Once I saw Julia smell one of the shirts, and an expression of immeasurable sorrow passed across her face.

Mary washed and folded the clothes. I'd try them on and say: The sleeves are too short. And Mary would reply: We'll hem the sleeves and fold them over and add buttons, easy. I'd try on a pair of pants and find that the waist was too big. Mary would laugh and say: You're all skin and bones, even with all those sandwiches you devour you're still all skin and bones. And then she'd say: You'd better not be playing soccer when our backs are turned! She was always laughing and joking and pinching me, but she'd stop laughing whenever she brought out one of Ilya's belts. She tightened the belt on me, but she could see it was no use, there weren't enough holes in the belt. I really was all skin and bones.

Then she'd scowl at me and ask where I learned to lie like that. Again, I'd swear that I wasn't playing soccer, but I could tell from her face that she didn't believe me. She'd feel the muscles on my legs and say: These here tell a different story. I said I ran a lot, I loved running, all of us ran a lot. And I'd kick the ground and push her hand away and say: Is running forbidden too?

When I think of those quarrels now, I see that she too acted like my mother. Mary. I remember in '82, when the planes were shelling West Beirut and the children in the neighborhood climbed onto the rooftops and said: this one hit the Hamra district, and that one hit Kola, and that one hit Mazra. I got hit too: with the measles. My face was covered with red dots and the doctor told me to keep away from people. The doctor warned my siblings and said adults could contract this type of measles too. Was it measles or smallpox? Were the dots red or black-brown? I'd come down with both of them: I had measles once, and smallpox once. You could call me a repository of diseases. I used to get nosebleeds sometimes too, but not very often. My nose would start bleeding whenever I played in the sun a lot. One time I got a nosebleed and sat down on the sidewalk in front of Mousa al-Zayyat's store (he used to sell us Arabic "ice cream" and claim it was the best in Achrafieh—it was a mix of water, ice, and coloring, and you could crunch it between your teeth). He came out and gave me a tissue, telling me to press down hard on my nose, right at the top of the bone, and he stretched out his hand—it was as small as a girl's, and also soft and damp, giving me the chills—and with his tiny fingers taught me how to press on the bone between my eyes to stop the bleeding. Raise your other hand, he said, and I raised it up high. Wait a bit now, he said, and the bleeding will stop. I asked him what would happen if it didn't stop. He replied: If the bleeding doesn't stop, you'll die. I remember the exact words he used: "You'll die." He said I'd die if the bleeding didn't stop. Years later, during the War of Elimination (1990), a burst of gunfire hit him in the liver.

While I was sick in '82, the bed shook beneath me whenever the planes flew over our house. Mary and my mother were worried about me. Whenever my mother was sleeping (if she'd taken her medication), Mary would be at my side. And when my father or Ilya came home (from the "lines" or the port or the Phalangist head-quarters), they'd approach my bed. Ilya wasn't scared of the measles because he'd had them when he was young and was immune now. He'd draw near, put his palm on my forehead, and say I was burn-ing up, smiling as he did so. My father would ask my sister when my fever had risen, and Mary would reach for the thermometer on the table by the bed, touch it, and say: Just a moment ago, or fifteen min-utes ago, or a half-hour ago. Are you wondering how I remember all of this as if it happened yesterday, and not twenty-six years ago?

I haven't forgotten the din of the warplanes. One time, as I was dragging my heavy head along the pillow (the itching sensation was awful, and they'd tied my hands so I wouldn't scratch my face), I saw a plane beyond the window, and watched the plane's shadow pass over me. The sun was shining on the metal, shining on the glistening silver. And the sound, the horrifying roar. Did I say I was only afraid of being kidnapped? Did I say the shelling wasn't paralyzing, and the roar of the planes wasn't terrifying? That wasn't true. I was afraid of many things. How could I not be afraid when I was so young and my drugged mother was always sleeping? How could I not feel fear when neither my father nor my brother ever stayed at home? And then there was Liliane, who was always crying in the bathroom. Whenever she heard shelling she'd rush to the bathroom, lock the door, and start crying. . . . When I think about Liliane, I think of how she spent fifteen years in the bathroom. Poor Liliane. Even when they were shelling West Beirut, she'd hear the explosions and think they were shelling East Beirut (it wasn't very far away, the only thing that separated us from them was the demarcation line) and rush to the bathroom. When I see Liliane's daughter now (did I tell you her name?—her name's Nathalie), I think I'm looking at Liliane, but there's one difference: that young girl doesn't look scared all the time.

Why is one person afraid when another isn't? Ilya left the house during the Mountain War in 1983. We knew that he and his friends were involved in the fighting, that they were moving around between the Shouf and Matn districts, but we didn't tell mother. When she asked us, we said he'd just gone out to buy bread. She'd fall asleep and when she woke up (she wasn't completely awake, her eyes would water as if there were rainclouds in them) she'd ask if Ilya had come back from the market, if he'd found any bread. And we'd say yes, he'd come back: "Here, eat this bite . . . Ilya just bought this fresh bread, he bought it just now." She'd ask us where he was. And we'd reply that he was on guard duty at Sassine Square, or that he'd gone to a friend's house, or that he was down at the port looking for our father. She'd ask us why we hadn't woken her. We'd say he'd sat beside her bed, waiting for her to wake up. Then my mother would eat a bit of *labneh* from my sister's hand and say she'd felt him, she'd felt his hand on her head.

Was Ilya not afraid? He told me countless stories about the Mountain War. A strange look would pass across his face when he spoke, and it felt like he was testing me, it felt like he wanted me to say something. But what? He asked me not to tell the family what he was up to. This stays between us, he'd say. But I didn't really understand what he meant by that. I understood half of it — and I thought I understood it all. Later, I'd remember those times when we were sitting on the roof, beneath the thatched shelter, and realize he'd meant something else entirely.

I clung to him back then. Before that, when I saw him taking care of mother, I'd begun to love him. No, I loved him from the beginning: he was my big brother, how could I not love him? Once, when I was out in the street, he hit a boy who had pushed me. That happened early on, before the Hundred Days War, or maybe shortly afterward, I'm not sure. Was it before '79? He used to provoke me in the house. He did it secretly, behind my parents' backs. There were times when he pushed me while my sisters were watching, but he never did that in front of mother or father. He kept going after me during those first few years — his mood would change suddenly, one moment he was an angel, the next a devil. But most of the time he was going after me. That's why I remember what happened so clearly, it was the very first time I really believed he loved me. Can you imagine? For years I'd been saying: That's my big brother, and of course he loves me like I love him, for years I'd been saying that without actually being sure of it — until I saw him hit that boy. We were playing in the street. Ilya was leaving a store and saw the boy push me, throw me to the ground, and kick me. I'd fallen on the asphalt, and out of the corner of my eye I caught sight of Ilya approaching quickly, a paper bag in his hand. I can still remember that coarse brown bag—can you believe it? We used to buy vegetables and put them in paper bags, before everyone started using plastic. He handed the bag to one of the kids, approached the boy who'd hit me, and said something to him. I was on the ground. I heard Ilya say the boy's name, and swear at him. I remember the swear word. And I remember how the boy screamed. Ilya grabbed his shirt, tearing it, and hit him. The boy's face started bleeding. I remember him screaming, "My tooth!" Is that memory real? I know all of it happened, and yet—after all this time, after everything I've learned and found out—I sometimes still mistrust my memories. But I remember Ilya lifting me off the ground, brushing the dirt off my clothes, and wiping my nose on his sleeve. I remember him looking at my shocked face and saying: "Don't play with them if you're going to cry."

But that was a rare occassion: it was unusual for someone to hit me. The people in the neighborhood loved me. Broadwell—a relative of the doctor who'd treated me and who was treating my mother—was the owner of a *ful* restaurant, and used to sometimes call out to me as I was walking by his store. "Come in," he'd say, before putting a bowl of hot fava beans on the table for me. He wouldn't take my money. I remember the first time he called me in: I was rolling a rubber tire (a car tire) on the sidewalk, guiding it with a large stick, but the tire kept falling over on its side. I'd lift it up again, and once more it would fall: it would roll in front of me as I took a step forward, but then topple over. I heard someone laughing, and when I looked up I saw him standing in the narrow doorway of his restaurant, wiping his hands on his white apron. As I looked into the restaurant (it was empty), and then up at him once more, he kept on laughing, and signaled for me to draw nearer.

"You're Felix's son, aren't you?"

He told me to leave the tire outside the door and the stick beside the tire. He was talking and laughing, and he pointed me to the sink inside and told me to wash my hands. Then he asked me what my name was. "Maroun," I said. "Do you like *ful*, Maroun?" he asked. I replied: Yes, I like the fava beans my mother makes, and the ones my sister Mary makes, but my sister Julia says the *ful* in restaurants is even more delicious. He went through the small door that led behind the stone counter: strangely shaped containers were lined up along the counter, and he was standing beneath a shelf covered with many jars of pickled vegetables. I'd seen those jars when I passed by outside the restaurant: red turnips, black eggplants, green cucumbers, and pickled green tomatoes. I looked at the jars of turnips in wonder and was struck by their color.

I ate the stewed fava beans while he sat at the table facing me, smoking his cigarette and looking out at the empty street as the sun shone on it. Did you like the *ful*? he asked me. This isn't *ful*, I replied, My sister always makes *ful* for me—is this really *ful*? I remember him laughing as I spoke. He used to love the way I talked. Don't repeat this to your sister, he replied, but *ful* from home isn't really *ful*. I boil the beans over a gentle flame all night long, I season them with my own mix of spices—it's a secret recipe, no one knows these things but the other *ful* makers. Each one has his own recipe, and when he grows old he calls his eldest son to him and tells him the secret.

I asked him if he'd told *his* eldest son the secret, and he said his son wasn't quite old enough yet. Then, I asked him if he'd tell his son when the time was right. He said he'd try, but his children were in America, and America was far away. He asked me if I knew where America was. I told him we were learning geography and history at the Sacred Hearts School: there was a big map hanging in the classroom, and I knew where America was: "America's right beside the classroom door." Everyone in our house heard that sentence. I don't know how my words reached home, but Mary knew I'd had Broadwell's *ful*, and anytime I asked her for some for breakfast she'd scowl and say: Go have your friend make it for you, I don't know how. (Years later, when Najwa was leaving for France via Cyprus and we went to say goodbye to her at the port in Jounieh, Ilya scolded Mary, who had tears in her eyes, and said: "Your sister's not going to America, France is closer than the classroom door.")

I loved that *ful* maker and used to call him "my uncle." Whenever I passed by his restaurant—which was near the Mayor's residence—and the restaurant was empty, he'd tell me to come inside. He always filled up an earthenware bowl for me. I can still see the white metal ladle dipping into the deep pot and emerging full of fava beans. And the steam—a cloud of steam would rise as soon as the cover was lifted from the pot, which had been boiling the whole time on the stove. I'd always look through the glass that separated us, and I'd stand on my tiptoes, trying to figure out what else he put into the small stone mortar where he mashed the garlic. And he'd laugh and refuse to reveal his secret. To this day I can't smell bitter oranges without thinking of that place: the white and red square tablecloths, the wood-paneled walls, the jars of turnips, the bunches of parsley and mint in plastic bottles, the smell of that seventy-year-old man who'd place the bowl of *ful* drenched in olive oil in front of me. And the smell of bitter oranges mixed with the smell of cumin.

His questions didn't bother me, even though they were strange. He'd ask me, for example, if I loved my mother. Or who I loved more, my mother or my father. The questions themselves weren't strange. Rather, his voice. Something in his voice would change when he asked me those questions. His tone wouldn't change, no, that's not it, I don't know how to explain it—words can't explain what someone is saying, what they're feeling. I noticed a strange gleam in his eyes when he asked me those questions. As if he were focusing his gaze on a single point on my face, as if he wanted to pierce me with that gaze and discover my secret. But what was the secret?

Ilya acted the same way sometimes. During the Hundred Days War, when the shelling was so intense that we were confined to the living room day and night, I'd catch him staring at me with that same strange look in his eyes: as if he wanted to peer into my depths. No, not my depths, I don't know how to say what I'm trying to say. No, it was as if he wanted to see something that he *couldn't* see—as if I were hiding another body within my own, a body beyond my body. I didn't think about those things back then, but maybe that was when I began to feel them (feel? think?). It's hard now to distinguish what I remember from what I imagine myself remembering. Everything blends together with the passing of time. I saw Ilya: tense, full of power, as if he were about to break the walls. My father forbade him from leaving the house. My father was out all the time, and my brother wasn't allowed to leave, even though no one could stop him from leaving. My brother never shut the door. He wasn't very big, and he wasn't tall either—he's still quite short, I'm taller than him now. He wasn't tall, but he had the strength of a bull. I remember him as a rough man who used to frighten strangers. He was small, but violent. Even today, even now that he's a "businessman," as he calls himself, even today there's a certain latent violence in the way he moves. He's short and, like the math teacher I mentioned to you, he only wears sandals. A businessman in sandals. He has three restaurants: one in Sadd al-

Bouchriya; another in downtown Beirut, which hasn't been doing so well lately; and one in Achrafieh, not far from our old house. He spends all his time on his feet, so he only wears sandals. But they're expensive sandals. He laughs whenever someone mentions them — he has countless pairs. He spends all his time standing in the doorway of one of the restaurants, smoking his Cuban cigars and keeping an eye on the business. He always wears a blue-jean jacket and black pants. He wears a khaki-colored shirt beneath his jacket, and during the summer he tosses the jacket over his shoulder. He's the same as always: power bursting out of him. He never sleeps more than five hours a night. He always stays at one of the restaurants until the chairs are put up on the tables. And he arrives before the workers, early in the morning, to keep an eye on the street cleaning. During the Hundred Days War he used to look at me and then at the picture hanging on the wall, the one with the black ribbon in the corner, and then he'd look at my mother, who was staring at him: she knew he was only staying at home for her sake, and she was sad because he was so full of anger and she didn't know what to say.

One time, he was fixing the living room door, the hinge of the door, that door led to the hallway and made an awful creaking sound whenever we opened it. Mary oiled it, and the oil worked for two days, but then it started creaking again. "We'll change it," Ilya said. He got out the toolbox and began taking the door off the hinge. He was unscrewing the old hinge when the shelling intensified, and bombs began falling behind the house, in the direction of the church. He stopped working and looked at Liliane. She was terrified of how he looked when he bit down on his lower lip. She was afraid of him, and she'd hide her face so he wouldn't raise his voice, even though he usually didn't raise his voice in front of mother. The shelling died down — or rather, it moved farther away — and so he went back to work on the old hinge and tried to take it off the door. At a certain moment he stopped trying. I saw the red liquid on his hand. He stood up holding the old door and smashed it against the wall, breaking it in two.

I remember how he used to come to school to get me whenever the shelling started. He came in an open-air jeep and drove the jeep into the middle of the schoolyard. No one could stop him. He'd take my heavy backpack from me and say, "Quickly, quickly." And in a flash we'd be back home. I remember the tires hissing on the asphalt amid the din of gunfire and screaming.

On one of those occasions I saw a man crawling on the sidewalk. He lifted his hand and looked up at us as we drove by in the jeep without stopping. I remember the blood on his face, and the filth on the walls. But he wasn't filthy.

That memory blends together with another one: We were in the safe room—not our living room, but the safe room of a building near our house, this one was underground—it was a storeroom, and now it's part of a supermarket—we were in the safe room and the power was out, only the emergency neon light was buzzing. The neon light was buzzing, and someone came in from outside, took off his coat, and started cleaning it. The smell of rain and gunpowder came in with him, and I heard him say that Broadwell—the *ful* maker—was splattered all over the tree in front of the store. In the Lebanese dialect, we use the word "bits" sometimes. He said, "His bits are splattered all over the tree." I didn't understand what he was saying at first, but then I understood: he said "his bits" were all over the cherry tree, "His bits are splattered over the whole tree." Over the whole tree.

We went there once the shelling stopped, once we could go outside again. A day or two had passed, I don't know how long exactly. They'd cleaned up the place, but you could see the marks the shell had left on the road and the gouges the shrapnel had left in the walls. The cherry tree's branches were broken. I used to watch it bloom in the spring, I used to gaze at its lovely white flowers. But I don't remember ever seeing any red cherries on it. Maybe it did bear cherries, and the kids who were bigger than me ate them while they were still green, I don't know. But I remember the white flowers, and I remember the boy I was sitting in the dimly-lit restaurant—I used to love that darkness, the darkness that hid me from prying eyes, hid me from my sister who would get upset if she passed by and saw me eating there, rather than at home, and I didn't want to make her angry, but at the same time I wanted to eat there, I loved eating there—I remember that boy dipping a piece of bread into the hot *ful* submerged in oil, and I remember him lifting that piece from the bowl to his mouth, how he ate onions and fresh mint and chopped tomatoes with the *ful*, and how he licked his fingers afterward. The *ful* maker would slice pickled turnips just for me, his fingers always steady against the knife, though they trembled whenever he struck a match to light a cigarette. I remember that boy sitting in the restaurant, and I remember the smoke rising from the cigarette, and I remember the sun casting light on the blooming cherry tree.

For a long time I couldn't pass by that sidewalk without looking at the tree. Years went by: new shops sprouted up, the sidewalk was widened, and the whole neighborhood changed. Many houses remained as they were, but others disappeared, replaced by tall buildings—yes, the whole street has changed: there are places that never see any sunlight now—they're covered in shadows from morning to night. And the cherry tree's gone. I don't know when they cut it down, but I still remember where it was.

Gone? Was it ever really there? There were a lot of us in the safe room: the residents of entire buildings would go down to that shelter when the shelling intensified. We knew the shriek of the rockets, and we knew which ones could pass through several floors of a building before exploding. Whenever we heard those shrieks in the sky, we'd run to that underground shelter. There were a lot of us down there. I remember the neon light buzzing, and I remember the man wiping the water from his hair and the coat hanging from his hand. I don't remember his voice, but the words—the traces of his words—still paint a picture in my mind, to this very day. And the others who were with me in the safe room, do they remember? Of course they do—at least some of them. Don't they? I'd like to know how they remember that incident.

I don't remember my father in the safe room. I remember Ilya pulling out heavy boxes and spreading things on the ground for my mother to sleep on. I remember a man with his family in the corner (the Taniyus family). He was holding his wife in one arm and his children in the other: all of them were trembling, and whenever they opened their eyes you could see the whites, even in the darkness you could still see the whites of their eyes. A moment came when darkness prevailed and the noise died down, when all you could hear was a prayer or a murmur, and also the snoring of an old woman in the corner of the room—in that darkness, no one could find her to shake her and stop the snoring. There were more than seventy people down there. Do I remember all their names? I used to know everyone in the neighborhood, and sometimes people from outside the neighborhood would come to that safe room as well: passersby who were caught off guard by the shelling, who'd rushed to the entrance of the building. There was a long staircase descending underground. I remember the lumps of hardened wax on the stairs, and I remember the colored plastic water bottles at the bottom of the stairs. I remember once, when I was half-asleep between my mother and sister, someone sparked their lighter in the darkness: I saw the light rise, and I saw a woman's face, round and yellow, her sweaty and disheveled blond hair around her ears—she was looking for a slipper, or something else she'd lost. I remember people swearing and praying, and I remember the crackling of a small transistor radio rounding out the night. I remember the man who looked after that building: he grabbed a cup of tea one day at sunset, went outside to inspect the street for a moment, and never came back.

I don't remember my father in the safe room. He'd disappear whenever the fighting started up, and sometimes he'd disappear before it started too. He'd only come home to eat or sleep. Mother's health would improve for short periods, and she'd get out of bed and wander from room to room. When that happened, white sheets would appear on the ground in the sitting room (where we never sat), with rows of delicious date cookies (*maamoul*) lined upon them. My father always wanted to celebrate whenever mother's health improved. I remember the first time I heard him say, as he was drinking his morning coffee, "The butcher's begun the slaughter." Was it the first time? I remember my sisters' joyful faces, and I remember my mother laughing and Ilya laughing too. That was an old expression in the family, an expression that meant something, as if it were the secret password to enter a palace they all knew about. It was new to me, though, because I was young, because I was a newcomer, and now I hardly know what it means anymore. My father got dressed and left without taking the car keys, and when he returned, there was a hunk of meat in his hand. I never saw my father in the kitchen except on occasions like those. My sister, Mary, brought him the wooden cutting board we usually used for vegetables and handed him the knife. Julia was there too, standing by the fridge and craning her neck to see. He cut out the raw black liver. He sliced off the fat and cut up the whole slab of meat himself, arranging the pieces on plates. Najwa cleaned the mint and peeled the onions. Julia got out some ice cubes. Ilya wasn't in the kitchen, he was helping mother set the table. Father was the only one who ever mixed the arrack, he'd mix it once we were all sitting at the table. It was morning, and we never ate meat in the morning — except for meat pastries (*manakish*) — but that morning we ate meat and drank arrack. He poured glasses for all of us. He even poured one glass for Liliane and me to share: he filled the glass with water and ice and put a single drop of arrack in it. We saw the drop fall into the water, saw the water suddenly turn milky white, then saw the white dissolve until the liquid was clear again — but Liliane said we were drinking arrack. Father clinked glasses with mother, Julia with Mary, Mary with Najwa, Najwa with Ilya. Ilya got up from his chair to lean across the table and clink glasses with mother, laughing. Liliane and I fought over our one glass, and wanted to toast with everyone. My mother prepared a bite for me: a small piece of onion, a fresh mint leaf from the tip of the branch (the "crown" of the mint), a piece of the black liver, and a piece of the lamb's white fat. She sprinkled some salt and cinnamon on it. I ate the morsel — I knew it was delicious, and I knew I loved it. But Liliane only ate olives. "Look," they told her, "look, why don't you eat like your brother?" I gazed at their faces and felt love fill the room, yet I could still make out a strange look in their eyes.

I told you I came down with measles once, and once with small-pox. Your temperature rises when you get sick, and because of the high fever your brain starts turning to mush, your mind starts imagining things. Scientists know this, they say Michelangelo was in that state while he was painting the dome of Saint Peter's Basilica. We have visions when we're sick, we see things we can't usually see. I have a memory from my illness: I'm wandering around the house by myself (I don't know where anyone else is—maybe they're at the school? maybe they've gone to the neighbors' house? maybe they're sleeping?), I'm wandering alone among the rooms, looking at the vase on the table, at the tin can on the dresser that Mary puts cookies in, at the clothes that Mary left on the bed, at the rocking chair where Ilya likes to sit when his friends visit; at the plastic covering the window that overlooks sandbags and a dry tree, at the cracked paint on the walls, at the spots where the paint hasn't cracked yet. . . . I'm alone in the house, wandering among the rooms as if walking on clouds. I see a doll on the ground and think about picking it up: I imagine myself bending over, but I don't actually do it because I'm tired and my head is heavy and the heaviness is gathering itself together into beads of sweat on my forehead, and so I continue walking as if something dark were calling me. (Many years later, while my mother was breathing her last on the bed in her room, my father came rushing home: he'd felt mother calling him.)

This is the memory: my cotton pajamas are drenched, they're clinging to my sick body while I, as if in a dream, walk to the living room and come to a halt in front of my dead brother's picture. I raise my eyes and stare into his face, considering the features of the face that looks like my own, focusing all the strength in my small head and trying to remember him while he was here, here in this living room where I'm standing, before they kidnapped and killed him.

WHO LIVES behind the demarcation line, in West Beirut? The English teacher answered our question in English: "Beasts and monsters," he said. I went with Antoine Tannouri — my best friend at the Sacred Hearts School — to the Violet Bookstore by the Hôtel Alexandre and got an English-Arabic dictionary to look up the two words. Who lives behind the demarcation line? Beasts and monsters. Killers and ghosts. Animals and demons. Antoine studied with me at the Nazareth School as well, but we weren't in the same section there, and we didn't stay friends. I switched to a new school and, coincidentally, he switched too, and we struck up our friendship again. We used to call Antoine "Bugs Bunny" because of his long ears, and he used to call me an ass and say he wasn't a rabbit, and then let out that loud laugh of his. He was constantly making fun of himself, and he was quick-witted — whenever he made fun of one of the teachers he always had us doubling over in laughter. He had a sharp mind and always got the highest grades, even though we never saw him study. He wore glasses with a frame made of black bone. His shirts were ironed, and smelled of soap.

We became fast friends at the Sacred Hearts School and continued our friendship at the American University (AUB). After that he moved to America for his graduate studies. Later, he married a woman from Texas and settled there. He has two sons: Robert and Timothy. Antoine (he goes by Anthony now) and I always helped each other out in trying times: we've stayed friends and often write each other e-mails, and sometimes he e-mails me pictures as well. Antoine knows my story. The Violet Bookstore I mentioned was burned down during the War of Liberation, or during the War of Elimination, I can't remember which. A shoe store is there now. Mary's house isn't far from the Hôtel Alexandre, and when I visit her I pass the place where the Violet Bookstore used to be and remember those two boys standing in the middle of the magazines and newspapers and notebooks, in the middle of the stationary and the few actual books they had there. I remember how we silently opened the dictionary and looked up the first word our teacher had uttered. We didn't know what letter it began with: a P or a B? Our teacher didn't pronounce things clearly.

English was taught as a third language in both the schools I attended. We focused on French and Arabic, and in the higher grades we focused exclusively on French. But during my senior year of high school, and even in my junior year, I'd begun paying more attention to the English lessons.

The war hadn't ended yet: Julia was thinking about leaving for Canada with her family, Najwa was planning to leave for Australia, and from time to time Mary would say that her husband's relatives in Venezuela were constantly writing them and inviting them to live in Caracas. Ilya was also thinking of leaving, and when the war reached the heart of East Beirut, he said, "We'll wait and see," putting his hand on his right leg, in the middle of his thigh, where he'd been hit by three bullets in the Battle of Bhamdoun (during the Mountain War) — and where a piece of shrapnel was still lodged, next to the bone.

My father was beyond the world back then. He was completely gone. Once, when there was fighting at Sassine Square, one of the soldiers fled into an alleyway behind our house. He was bleeding from his back and his neck, and couldn't figure out how to put pressure on both wounds with his hands. He dropped his gun so that his hands were free, but he couldn't block both wounds. Ilya said afterward that father had told him about that. I'd never heard my father tell any stories or provide any details, but Ilya said father had told him, and maybe Ilya embellished the story a bit.

My father was bringing the cages in from the balcony. He was worried about the birds, about the canaries, not because of the gunfire but because of the noise. Gunfire never hit that side of the house when there was fighting. They didn't fight on that side. There were other periods when the balcony was exposed to shrapnel, but not back then. Ilya says that father saw the soldier from above: sometimes the soldier used both his hands to try to stop the bleeding in his neck, and sometimes he used his hands to stop the bleeding in his back, near his kidney. One hand wasn't enough. The blood was pouring out of him, and his clothes were soaked black. Our neighbor yelled at him to go to the hospital.

While I was listening to Ilya speak, I remembered the time I went to the demarcation line with Antoine. We slipped out of school and jumped over the fence behind the girls' playground. We hid our backpacks in a half-wrecked house that had burned down, and went off on our journey. A large part of the road was sunk in shadows because of the tall curtain of dust to the left of us: sniper fire was coming from over there. Antoine had relatives who lived at the end of Lebanon Street, in the Tabaris district. They only used half of the rooms: there were piles of sandbags and drums full of stones in the rooms facing West Beirut.

To this day, my whole body recoils whenever I think about that trip to the demarcation line. We looked ahead of us and tried to make out the features of the burned buildings in the distance, and asked ourselves how they could live over there with all the shattered windows, in buildings riddled with bullets and shrapnel—how did they live in those black buildings? We didn't know, we couldn't imagine it, we couldn't see, as we peered out fearfully from our vantage point in the shade of that cold wall of dust, the sweat soaking our shirts, our hearts beating in our mouths—no, we couldn't see what was beyond the wrecked buildings: the buildings looked like a range of mountains made of gray concrete and black holes, a chain that rose and fell (the tops of some of the buildings were gone). We couldn't see beyond those mountains. When I remember that distant day, two images come to mind: the first is the image of those buildings, and in my imagination I saw, behind them, more buildings that looked just like them, all black and wrecked and eaten away by the shelling, rows upon rows of buildings, all of them like that, and all of them with people inside, but we couldn't see any people from where we were. That's the first image. The second image: the black corpse of a woman. She wasn't black. She was white. But most of her body had turned a different color, almost black. Antoine saw her first. We were hiding among the ruins, taking care not to get mud on our shoes, and from time to time we'd bend down to gather some of the (empty) bullet casings. . . . I said something about the smell before Antoine saw the woman lying there, abandoned among the wrecked wooden boxes of ammo. The stench was awful, and we assumed she came from the other city. (Some of the girls in our class said they'd seen, in their dreams, "those people" sneaking in at night from behind the sandbags, and that they were humans just like everyone else, just like us, except their faces were longer and looked like the faces of dogs, and they had long fingernails, and they kidnapped young children from their families and then screamed and rushed away, leaving no trace but their strange smell.)

Antoine froze in fear, pointing at the woman. Her clothes were tatters, or what was left of tatters: they were muddy and charred black, like pieces of coal, as if they weren't made of cloth. I saw something green and blue and black swimming in a small pit beside her. The pit was full of a thick and strangely colored liquid, and a small sharp-smelling cloud was rising from the hissing liquid. The woman's mouth was open, her teeth white against her black mouth.

I don't know who she was, and I don't know who killed her and left her there. Maybe she'd been exploring the demarcation line like us when a bullet got her. Or had she snuck in from the other side? I don't know who she was, I only saw her for a moment or two (I can't say how long exactly) before Antoine and I started back, we started back without finishing our journey, retracing our steps. We didn't speak while we walked, we didn't speak while we ran, we didn't speak when we started walking again. We didn't speak at all. We returned to the burned-down house and got our backpacks. We took turns helping each other with the backpacks so the straps wouldn't break: he helped me put mine on, and I helped him with his. I don't remember us talking. Maybe one of us said something, but I can't remember a single word now. There was a point on the road where we went our separate ways: he to his house, and I to mine. I remember that point now: there was an old broken-down car on the side of the road, it was covered in dirt and bird drop-pings. There's an acidic substance in bird droppings that eats away at paint: the paint on this car was cracked everywhere, and the whole car was in awful shape, all its tires were flat. A thick layer of dust covered its windows, and we used to write swear words or funny expressions on them. I remember Antoine standing there, by the old car: there were people and other cars and passersby all around us, but we didn't hear or see any of that. We wanted to hear it, we wanted to see it — but how?

Around the same time we took that trip to the demarcation line,

Ilya disappeared from the house. He began going to the front lines a lot, and the first time he came back from the mountain, from Mount Lebanon — while the battles were still going on there — I could tell he was no longer himself. He'd suddenly become like my father. I don't know how to explain this, it all seems a bit silly, it seems silly that someone could change from one day to the next, or over a couple weeks, the way that . . . Listen, none of that matters. That's how Ilya looked when he started going to the lines: he looked like he was no longer himself.

It's not that he was different around us, or that he became violent (although some time after that, after my mother passed away, he said something horrible to Najwa, and I don't think Najwa, to this day, has ever forgiven him). No, it's the opposite: when he came home he'd sit on the bed by my mother's side and talk to her and run his fingers through her hair. And when we sat down for dinner he'd joke around with Julia and Mary, and with Najwa and Liliane, and with me, and he'd often stand up to get something from the fridge and say, "Each of us should pull our own weight" — he wouldn't let anyone bring him anything. He never said anything about the battles when we were at the table, and instead, he'd say something like, "We sat at the barricades all day and nothing happened." But his voice — the tone of his voice, his smile — said something different, that he never sat at the barricades. When my mother joined us for dinner, he always sat beside her, or she'd come and sit by him. He'd feed her and she'd laugh and say, "I'm your mother, don't you have any manners?" And then she'd kiss his head. She'd kiss his head and he would kiss hers. We rarely saw my father and brother at the same time. We knew they always met up: the two of them met all over the place, but they rarely got together at the house (at our house) during the Mountain War.

Ilya didn't talk about the war in front of my mother or my sisters, but, later on, I learned he sometimes told things to Julia, and sometimes to Najwa. After he came back home, after he was wounded in the thigh, and after his recovery, I heard a lot of stories from him. Those stories transformed him, once again, before my very eyes: he no longer looked like my father when he spoke. He looked like my father at other times: when he was feeding my mother, or joking around with my sisters, or grabbing a beer from the fridge, opening it and tossing the cap into the sink and turning back toward us. And he looked like my father when he came through the door and set the weapons down on the chair, a smile appearing on his dark, weary face: it was as if Ilya were changing his countenance for our sake. Those were the moments when he looked like my father. But when he told stories about the attacks and the defensive lines, about the raids and the massacres, he no longer looked like my father. He often said that it was similar to what had happened at such and such a place and at such and such a time, and he often brought my father into the story, wanting me to understand that he was just like my father, and that father was just like him, that they were carbon copies of one another. . . . When he saw I wasn't listening anymore, or when he noticed he was losing me, he'd change the subject. He'd tell me, for example, that one of his friends had been killed by mistake, he wasn't killed in any of the battles, but he didn't notice a roadblock while he was on his way home, half-drunk, and they gunned him down right here: his own friends gunned him down and killed him without realizing who it was. "He always used to tell us he never got drunk, he said he could drink a whole barrel of whisky without getting drunk. Look at the poor guy now."

Why did his stories unsettle me? Was it the stories themselves? My guess is that it wasn't the stories, but rather the look in his eyes—yes, I think that's right. He used to give me a look I didn't understand. I often saw that look in his eyes, but I never understood why he was staring at me like that. He'd be describing something, for example, and then he'd suddenly focus his gaze on a specific point on my face, burning a hole into me. I've told you something like that before. I'm repeating something I've already said, aren't I? I think I am.

That strange feeling stayed with me for years: I was confronted with that same difficult situation at different points in my life, and I could never voice my thoughts. I wanted to ask Ilya, "Why do you look at me like that?" But I didn't know what to say, I didn't know how to explain it, and I didn't know how to stop him from looking at me like that. There was a lot I didn't know. . . . I felt that terrifying impotence over and over again. Once I even caught my mother looking at me like that when I wasn't paying attention. She'd been asleep, or half asleep, and I was sitting on the edge of the bed and reading a book. She always wanted one of us to be there, she didn't like spending too much time alone in the bed. I was reading my book, and from time to time I'd look up at something on the nightstand (the framed picture of Saint Charbel, the cup of water, the watch with the silver dial and leather band), or I'd look at my mother's face, sunk in peaceful sleep. I loved that sleeping face, and I loved watching it. A strange calm would come over me whenever I looked at it. I was reading when I felt her gaze bearing down on me: I turned around slowly and saw that strange look. When she noticed I'd seen her, she closed her eyes. I haven't forgotten that moment. I'll never forget that moment. Something deep within me broke when I saw that look in my mother's eyes.

The strange thing is that I never—not in my whole life— saw anything like that in my father's eyes. Don't you think that's strange? Not once did I catch that look in my father's eyes. Never. Najwa says father's a mystery, she says she doesn't love him, she says she *really* doesn't love him, but she can't say she hates him either. "My father's a mystery," she says. And she also says: "Your father's a mystery." Even though we now know (and she knew from the beginning) that he's not really my father.

But he *is* my father. Isn't he my father? I remember when he hit Ilya with his cane. Ilya had been using the cane because of his wounded leg. He couldn't walk without it. He was afraid he'd become a cripple. One of the doctors told him the likelihood of that happening was small, but that it *was* a remote possibility because of the piece of shrapnel still in his thigh. The piece had lodged in the bone and was in a tricky spot to get to: he could lose his leg if they tried to remove it and the operation failed. Ilya told me about his friend who'd lost a leg. I knew him, I often saw him with Ilya in Haghoub Manukian's red Chevy, which Haghoub claimed he'd plundered from "the most important military leader in West Beirut," but that car wasn't from the war. Ilya frequently got together with his friend: they'd meet up at an underground casino or at a whorehouse or at the demarcation line (the story was different each time), and they played roulette. They played roulette or poker or hearts or seven and a half (the story was different each time). His friend was running through some land outside the village of Souk al-Gharb when he stepped on a mine. Did he step on it, or was it the person running beside him? Someone stepped on the mine and Ilya's friend was launched through the air, and when he landed back on the ground he discovered he'd lost his leg. Then he passed out. He used to play soccer, Ilya said. And he said that's what bothered him the most: he'd no longer be able to play. In the hospital, he'd stand on his crutches and jump on his one leg and ask for a ball so he could play in the corridor.

My father wasn't angry about Ilya's story, but he did get angry about the gold bracelets: Ilya had brought home some "spoils of war." My father took the cane from him. He asked him for "the stick" and lifted it into the air. We didn't know what he was doing, his voice didn't change when he asked for the stick, and we couldn't tell he was fuming inside. Then he brought it down hard on Ilya's arm — as I tell you all this, I can almost hear it snapping against the bone — I can almost hear the snapping of the cane, and the venomous sentence that came out of his mouth: "You're stealing, you son-of-a-bitch!"

We never saw any spoils of war in the house after that. That memory is linked to another one from the period following my mother's passing. I was overcome with grief, and whenever the teacher asked me a question in class I was unable to reply — some kind of speechlessness came over me after her death. She died while I was sitting next to her on the bed. She was crying as she looked at me. I'll never forget her face as she was dying. After that, I lost my appetite. I didn't even drink any water. In class, I listened and I didn't. I saw the letters and numbers on the board but didn't know what they were. I heard the chalk, the awful scratching, the scraping. I heard the chalk break. I heard someone break a fingernail. I saw birds flying outside the classroom window. I saw a line of pine trees. I saw the yellow pollen rise up from the branches. I saw the dry pinecones fall onto the balcony and hop like squirrels before dropping onto the playground. I saw faces, and I didn't. The winds blew, the rains fell. The clouds moved off and the weather cleared. I didn't feel any of it. The wheel of the seasons turned, but I was outside all of it. I was hollow. The teacher would ask me a question and I'd say nothing, then I'd hear laughter (were they laughing? I'm not sure), and then silence once more. Later, I stopped going to school, though I left the house with my books like I did every morning. I took the sandwich Mary wrapped in red paper for me, but I didn't go to school. I'd walk around the neighborhood, I'd take roads where the neighbors wouldn't see me, and I'd go somewhere far away. Far away from what? Where did I go? I never paid attention to where I went. Once I found myself in a part of the city that was packed with shops: a strange place I'd never been to before. I heard a language I did and did not understand. I stood there a long time in confusion, then I remembered. The language came back to me, and I saw the signs above the shops. I stood there looking at the passersby, eating my sandwich. I can still remember what the sandwich was: oil and *za'atar* with cabbage.

The human mind is unfathomable—how can I remember that sandwich? Why did my mind hold onto that detail but get rid of all the others? I don't remember, for example, what streets I took that day as I walked aimlessly from Sioufi to Burj Hammoud. I don't remember them at all. Did I take al-Karam? Al-Tawaheen Street? How did I get to Burj Hammoud? I don't remember. And why did Armenian sound like such an alien language to me? (We had Armenian neighbors in Sioufi. I had Armenian friends at school. I heard them talk all the time. I knew a lot of the words. Despite all that, I thought I was on another planet when I heard them speak that day.)

I stood there nibbling on my sandwich, holding my books under my arm, which were bound together by a large elastic strap (at school, you do away with your backpack once you get a bit older—backpacks are for the younger kids—and you wrap your books and notebooks together with an elastic strap . . . and when you're older still, you do away with the books altogether and go to school with just a single notebook with a blue Bic pen in the spiral binding).

I stood in the labyrinth that was the Armenian quarter, I stood there in the din of the strange words and cars, in the middle of strange faces and buildings and stores, I stood there eating my sandwich with tears streaming down my face. I didn't realize I was crying. A man approached and said my name. He looked right at me, and I couldn't understand how he knew my name. His face was swimming, and the cars passing on the street were swimming too, and so were the electric lamps lighting up the signs of the shops and the goods in the windows. I looked at the man and waited for the tears to pass.

"You're Felix's son. What are you doing here?"

The man took me by the arm and led me into his store. He sat me down on a chair. The place was full of refrigerators. He opened up one of them and took out a pitcher of water. He poured me a cup and asked if I was okay. I thanked him for the water. I'd dried my eyes on my sleeve as he was taking the water out of the fridge. I'd dried my eyes as I was walking with him into the store. I was still trying to dry my eyes as I sat there on the chair, and when he poured me a cup of water and asked if I was okay, I thanked him for the water.

I thanked him for the water and said his name (I knew him, he lived by the Halw house, at the end of Sioufi Street—I knew him and he knew us). I also said I was late for school. Before I left his store (as I was leaving, as I was stepping across the threshold), he said: "Maroun, look after yourself, and look after your father, OK? I've always said it, your father Felix is a good man. He never gets his hands dirty. Felix is a good man."

Did he say those words? Did he say something along those lines? I told you our minds are strange. One of the things I've always found hard to remember is the order of words. I remember images—why wouldn't I remember them? Why would you forget anything you see in your life, anything at all? When you see it, it leaves an imprint in your mind, right? And since it's been imprinted in your mind, it's in there somewhere. It's there in your head, right? In your memory, and if you look for it, you should be able to find it. I told you I don't remember the streets I took that day from Sioufi to Burj Hammoud.

But if I tried, if I really tried hard, wouldn't I remember? Maybe I wouldn't. That's trickier than remembering a single image, for example the image of the washing machines and refrigerators in the store, and the pitcher of water being taken out of one the fridges. But that's just one image. It's not a series of images. Whereas the route from Sioufi to Burj Hammoud is a series, and is more prone to being forgotten. It's harder to remember a whole series. But I think my trouble remembering is related to my state of mind that day: I was miserable, and although I was looking straight ahead, I couldn't see a thing. That's why I forgot which streets I took, that's why I suddenly found myself in a strange place, listening to a strange language. I didn't see what my eyes were seeing. That's why I forgot.

I'm telling you this story because it's linked with Ilya getting hit on the arm with the cane. I heard words like that a lot at my mother's funeral, and then at my father's. I used to think the people in the neighborhood loved and feared my father at the same time. But words like those, which I heard here and there, pointed me to a truth I hadn't given sufficient thought to: they also loved him because he never stole, he never "got his hands dirty."

And the blood on his hands? My father's not here and I can't ask him. I studied mechanical engineering in college. Don't ask me why I chose that subject. The plan was to study engineering, some type of engineering: computer engineering, electrical, mechanical, civil, architectural—it didn't matter. I was accepted into mechanical, so that's what I studied. We could take an elective course the first semester, we could take any course we wanted from the arts and sciences division, not from the engineering school—you know how AUB is. I loved the upper floors of the university, not the lower ones. Engineering was in the basement, but I used to love climbing the steps to my elective class.

I took a class in the English literature department: we studied two of Shakespeare's plays. I'd only ever read Shakespeare's sonnets. The professor had a white beard, he smoked Galleon cigarettes, and his hands were massive, as if he'd worked on the land his whole life. He stood in front of the class, acting out scenes from those two plays, and as he acted them out, I thought back to things long past: my father suffered his second heart attack during those first few weeks I lived on campus.

I've already told you about the operation at the Rizq Hospital: that was after his first heart attack. If it hadn't been for the heart attack, the doctor wouldn't have known about the tumor in his brain. The heart attack was how they found the tumor. Before that, my father had been going to the optometrist because he'd begun to lose sight in his left eye. The optometrist was clueless — he couldn't figure out what was happening. If he'd paid closer attention, he could have spared my father that first heart attack.

But the operation, though it saved my father's life, wasn't enough. They removed part of the tumor, but it was impossible to extract all of it — that would have damaged some of the cranial nerves and brain tissue. After the surgery, the doctor explained everything he'd done. They used delicate instruments, like tiny tongs, to gather up the malignant matter and remove it. They removed one tiny piece after another, moment after moment. The doctor worked on my father's brain for three hours without stopping, until his hand couldn't do it anymore. He removed the tumor bit by bit by bit. It was a mix of soft gelatinous matter and membranes and arteries: the difficulty of the surgery was the tumor's location in the middle of a bunch of healthy nerves, in the cerebral cortex. The cancer had spread through the nerves like a system of roots. The slightest mistake would wreck the patient.

The first operation was related to what Ilya told me that night: when he was describing the day father went out in his slippers to identify my little brother's body in the Hôtel-Dieu morgue, when he said, "He hit his head with his own hand," I felt a throbbing in my brain. It was as if I were the one lying on my back beneath the glaring white lights, there, behind the closed doors. And as if my father, while he was punching his head on that distant day (before I became a part of his world), had given himself that deadly disease without realizing it.

That last thought might not be true. I believe it's true now, but I don't think it's what was going through my mind in the Rizq Hospital that night. I can remember what I felt as I listened to Ilya talk: I felt my head split in two and I wanted—sitting in that waiting room—to grab at my head and keep it from splitting open. That's what I felt: I, like my father, had a tumor in my brain. I didn't have any thoughts beyond that. That's as far as I got.

My father didn't regain sight in the one eye after the first operation. In spite of that, more than one doctor assured us they considered the operation a success. Yes, the nerve was damaged, yes, the eye had gone out, but they still considered the operation a success: the tumor had been threatening more than just one nerve. The tumor had threatened to paralyze my father, and he had been saved from paralysis, even if he could only see out of one eye. His other eyelid was drooping now, and suddenly he seemed to have aged ten years in a single day.

He could only see out of his right eye. It was with that right eye that he watched me enter the house, my face dark, as I came back from Khalil Sufayr's, from the home of Hilda's father.

I told you about her. I'll get to that part of my story. But I'm trying, to the best of my ability, to stick to a logical order. It's important to have some order. My sister says I've got a knack for it. She might be right: in the entire dorm at AUB, my room was the only one that didn't look like a garbage dump.

It was the middle of the Mountain War. During Ilya's convalescence, while he was hanging out late into the night with his friends on the roof, his thigh wrapped in gauze, Najwa began training with the women Phalangist fighters in the fields near the town of Bikfaya, and then in the woods around Bsharri. She learned how to fire rocket-propelled grenades in the shade of the cedars: she trained with an RPG-7. When she came back carrying weapons that the enemy had carried (they were plunder), she told us the war was cruel and hard, and not everyone could bear it. Ilya asked her if she'd be willing to kill. Najwa replied that she had a friend who was several years younger, and in the training in Bsharri she saw her friend wearing ammunition belts around her neck and jumping over barricades and lying on her stomach behind a heavy *Dushka* machine gun (it was Jeannette Sawaya, who was later killed in the clashes that followed the "Tripartite Agreement"). Najwa said she saw her friend scream as she fired the *Dushka*, and that the bullets tore through stones and trees on the strip of land across the way. Her friend was young—maybe thirteen—but terrifying. She said that as her friend was holding onto the barrel of the *Dushka* to change the ammunition, the lead of the gun clung to the flesh of her fingers. She put some oil on her fingers and wrapped her hand in gauze, and you couldn't see a single tear in her eyes. Ilya asked her why she'd gone to train if she was going to be so afraid. Najwa said she wasn't afraid, she hadn't said anything about fear.

Was she afraid? Ilya conducted my own training on the roof, while drinking arrack and munching on pickles. He showed me how to disassemble a weapon and clean it, and how to put it back together. He taught me how to get the ammunition clips ready. And he took me to the old playground and taught me how to shoot. At night on the roof, he was laughing half-drunk and oiling the spring of the sniper rifle while giving me lessons (if the wind is blowing in this direction, then you've got to aim like this; and if you're firing an RPG-7, then you've got to remember that it's a strange type of rocket, light in the back but heavy up front, and a strong wind will blow it off course ... the gun you've got now will compensate for the wind if you aim it like this—you've got to shoot to the side of the target and the wind will take the bullet straight to its mark), beneath the thatched shelter where my father, years later, after the loss of my mother, hung up the canary cages and sat as though he'd become half a man, Ilya talked and laughed and forgot about what happened on Mount Lebanon and how the Mountain War ended ... Even though East Beirut was full of refugees then, and half his friends had been lost in the valleys or were lying wounded in the hospitals. He laughed and told me I should pay attention. Who knows? he said: One day you might be forced to carry a weapon, for wars like this never end, and you might lose a battle but not the war: you win some battles and you lose some, and it will keep on going and going until one of us wipes out the other, it's us or them, but we've been here for centuries and aren't going anywhere. He kept on talking and drinking, and then he lay down on the foam mattress and fell asleep.

Sometimes the two of us weren't alone. A friend of his would join us up there occasionally—he came by a lot back then, and whenever he visited he'd bring some pastrami. I don't know how I've forgotten his name—I rarely forget names, but I've forgotten his. He'd fought alongside Ilya on the mountain. He was tall, very tall, unlike Ilya. He had curly black hair, and whenever he played cards he'd run his fingers through his hair as if to scratch his brain. One time the two of us were alone up there, just me and him—Ilya was snoring, fast asleep. He lit one of his cigarettes for me and said, "Let's go for a walk." We walked to the edge of the roof, behind the water tank. From there we could see the lights of the Dawra district and those of the opposite hills. In the Bay of Dawra, the lights of an anchored ship were glistening on the dark surface of the water. That man whose name I've forgotten told me a story without once raising his voice: They were attacking a village in a valley by Mount Lebanon, a small village with just a handful of homes. He didn't know why they were attacking it or who gave the order, but he went with Ilya into a small house. "You wouldn't believe what a primitive village it was! You wouldn't believe that villages like that are still around these days. They were still growing silkworms, can you believe it? And they had wooden spoons! They fled when we started firing. People normally don't flee. But that night they did. Ilya saw a boy hiding behind some sheep. The boy came out with a gun in his hand, and he shot Ilya. I asked Ilya how he managed to do that, why he let the boy shoot him. Do you know what he said? He'd hesitated, he couldn't shoot the boy. Why? I asked. Why'd you let that happen? What were you thinking? Do you know what he told me? Do you know what your brother said? He said: I was thinking about Maroun."

I don't know why the man told me this story. I looked at his face and saw that he was gazing at a point in the distance: maybe he was looking at the boat anchored in the bay, or maybe he was looking at the lights glistening on the sea. His face revealed nothing. (Am I imagining that now? Am I remembering it or imagining it? And how can I tell the difference? Memory's a massive reservoir, it's a deep well, it's got layers upon layers upon layers—what does it bury, and what doesn't it?)

Najwa never fought in the war. She took part in another training drill—how to plant mines—but she never went to war. When we reminded her later of her combat training, she'd just laugh and say it was madness, a hereditary madness. Was it hereditary? I remember this image, after father struck Ilya on the arm: Ilya standing in the living room at night. The lamp in the room had been turned off, but some light was coming in from the window or from another room, and I saw Ilya's ghost standing there, the white gauze on his leg visible in the darkness. Was he standing without the cane? I don't remember. But I remember his leg wrapped in white gauze, and I knew he was looking at the picture on the wall. What was he doing? Talking to the picture? What was he saying?

That was the period when George Sader came and asked for my sister Julia's hand. He had studied law and had been an intern at the Iddah firm, but he never practiced. He worked at the Fattal Group after abandoning law, and in the darkest days of the war he started his own import-export business and also began trading currency. His mother was related to my mother, and they'd visit our house on special occasions, and my mother, before she fell ill, often took my sisters to go visit their home. My father talked to Julia about it. I remember his words: "It's your decision. This is your life, and it's your choice, and I'm your father and I'll support you either way."

Ilya said, "There are a lot of men who want to . . ."

My father silenced him: "I didn't ask you, Ilya, I asked your sister. The man came and asked for *her* hand, not yours."

My sister's face was serene, and her eyes were unclouded as she looked at my father: "I've grown up, father, and I don't want to wait any longer. He's a good man, and we've become close — why would I say no?"

"Congratulations," my father replied.

During their engagement, the man came every day at sunset to sit with my sister in the living room. My mother would sit with them a little while, and so would Mary and Najwa, and also Liliane. I'd come in, shake hands with him, and we'd exchange a few words before I went out again. Ilya did the same. The man would sometimes bring a box of baklava with him, and sometimes a cake from

Chocolat Nora. One time he brought us a gift from his family (he said it was from his mother)—a sealed glass jar filled with a strangely colored jam. It looked like apricot jam or peach jam, but it smelled different. He said they only make that jam on Mount Lebanon, and that it's made from pumpkins. It was yellow (the color of lemons), and when you lifted up your fork you could see the fibrous strands. I'll never forget that evening: as I ate the strange jam, I felt a silent weeping rise from my depths. I was alone in the kitchen, standing at the white sink, and the plate was in the sink. I ate another forkful as the sweet smell (what was that smell?) filled my nose (it filled my head, it filled my heart, I knew that smell, I knew this food, the curious substance melted on my tongue, it melted between my teeth, and a strange dark emotion welled up inside me). I haven't forgotten how I stood all alone in the kitchen while the light from the lamp fell on the sink's tiles, illuminating the yellow substance in the glass jar. What was I remembering at that moment?

Years later, as Khalil Sufayr smiled and said what he had to say to me, as the vast living room in his vast house closed in on my body, crushing me with its carpets and paintings and curiosities, its chandeliers still glistening in the light of the vanishing sun, I felt the same food on the roof of my mouth: after we'd eaten cold and flavorless kibbeh from a tray, the servant had brought us some jam.

The first time I had that jam, a river of light burst from my heart. The second time (as I looked at that face clouding over, even as a yellow smile appeared on it), darkness struck my eyes, and I begged to vanish from the world. Certain memories evoke certain other ones—they're joined by strings invisible yet real.

When the army left West Beirut in the winter of '84, Najwa came home from her job at the Zahrat al-Ihsan School and told us, as she put her books and papers and quizzes on the dining room table (the table had become her desk), that she wouldn't be staying in this country. "Every day we say this war needs to end, and every day there's more destruction—it won't end." Six years after she spoke those words, they shelled the presidential palace and attacked East Beirut, and the war ended—but she wasn't here. She was in Paris. On the phone, she asked me how things were and asked about my father's health. I heard her distant voice and I remembered how she used to sit with Julia and Julia's fiancé in the living room: the couple would sit on the sofa beneath the picture with the black ribbon, and Najwa would sit on the sofa, facing the picture. (At night that velvet sofa turned into her bed. She'd put a cotton sheet on it—she was allergic to the velvet, hives appeared all over her skin whenever she slept directly on it—and wrap herself up in a blanket, but she'd never use a pillow, instead she'd just fold her hand beneath her head.) I'd walk past in the hallway on my way out of the house and catch a glimpse of her sitting there, her fingers interlaced on her knees. What was she looking at? Was she looking at Julia and her fiancé, or at my little brother's picture? I don't know.

On the phone, while I was listening to her speak a mixture of Arabic, French, and English, I wanted to ask her if she remembered how she used to drag me with her to the gates of the embassies: there was a period in the second half of the '80s when we (just Najwa and I) used to wake up at dawn, drink our coffee, and then grab a bottle of water and make the rounds of the embassies. One day we'd go to the French Embassy, and the next day to the Canadian one, and the following day to the Australian. And then to the Swiss Embassy, and to the Dutch, British, and New Zealand embassies. There wasn't a single embassy whose gate we didn't sit in front of—and after they'd said a few words to us (or sometimes they wouldn't even say anything), they'd give us some forms and we'd fill out the forms, hand them in, and then they'd give us imaginary appointments. And sometimes we'd actually get a meeting. Then nothing would happen. They'd take our phone number, or they wouldn't take it. And nothing would happen. And when the Australian Embassy finally accepted Najwa's application, she changed her mind. I asked her why we'd been standing in all those lines. Why had we stood there and eaten all that melting chocolate while we waited in the hot sun? And she replied: "Now we know it's possible to leave."

Was it possible to leave? Would *I* leave one day? I'm still standing there, in the old kitchen of the Achrafieh house, raising the fork with pumpkin jam and bringing my lips to the fork: the thick substance melts in my mouth as I close my eyes, and incomprehensible memories surge in my depths—what's down there? Gardens or swamps? A sea or a desert? The memories flood over, images I don't understand, I don't know where they've come from, and I don't know what's happening to me. Do you remember that woman, the one with the round face and the damp blond hair, do you remember that yellow face? Didn't I tell you that while I was half asleep in the safe room I saw the spark of a lighter in the darkness, and I saw a yellow face in that light (beneath the yellow circle that looked like a halo)? Do you remember? In my dreams, shortly after George Sader began coming to our house, I started seeing that woman, but I didn't know why. Who was she? Why did I look at her like that? Why was she so important to me? I didn't know her face from the neighborhood. With the exception of this dark memory from that night in the safe room, I can't remember ever having seen the woman's face. Had I seen her in a dream that night, while I slept, covered by a sheet, between my mother and my sisters?

In college, as I studied Saint Augustine (I took that course in my second semester, it too was elective) and read about how memory is a vast palace with many rooms, how there are corridors and cellars beneath the palace, I thought of my mother sitting in the living room, her legs propped up on the small table (we'd moved father's stone ashtray out of the living room: there was no need for it, since Julia's fiancé didn't smoke). I saw my mother, a white sheet covering her legs, and I saw the branches Julia had sewn onto the sheet with green thread. Mary entered carrying cups of lemonade on a tray while my mother gazed at her with that look of love that flooded the world. Mary sat down beside her. Julia and her fiancé were sitting across from them, drinking the lemonade (the cups were cold, covered in condensation — Julia wrapped a Kleenex around her fiancé's cup). Mary dipped some cake into the lemonade and put it on a plate in front of my mother, on the wooden arm of the sofa.

I've told you about my unsettling dreams: a strange series of dreams began disrupting my sleep back then, when Julia was preparing for her wedding. The same dream kept repeating, with some small detail changing each time. That would last a while, then a new dream would come. And then this new dream would be a bit different each time, too. And sometimes the old dream would come back, or the two dreams would blend together. Or a third dream would blend in with the other two, or not blend in and appear as an entirely separate dream, but then afterward I'd think it was like the two previous dreams. It's not easy for me to remember all the details. But I do remember a number of those dreams and nightmares. What I remember most vividly is the impression they left in my mind, the feeling of disarray and confusion, of incomprehension.

I didn't know what was happening. The nightmares became so bad that they stayed with me even after I'd woken up. Do you know what I saw? I saw my father attacking me with a knife. Was it my father, or Ilya, or Najwa? I don't know. The face kept changing. I didn't know why I was being attacked, I hadn't done anything. In another nightmare I was on the roof of the house, or on the roof of the school, and I saw Ilya's face darken as he lifted something heavy off the ground and threw it at me (I don't know what it was, but it was heavy). He was trying to kill me, and I couldn't move. I tried to get away, but I was glued to the ground. I'd wake up terrified, my heart pounding, just as the object was about to hit me: I didn't die in those nightmares, but I was a hair's breadth away from it.

On the other hand, I also had "dreams" that weren't nightmares, but these confused me too: I'd see a wooden door that had been painted green. The door had a brass knocker that looked like a claw. I'd hear a familiar voice repeat a name in my ear and ask me to do something (the voice was familiar in the dream, but when I woke up and tried to remember whose it was, I couldn't). In the dream I knew the voice was saying my name, but it didn't say "Maroun," it called me something else, a word I knew was my name, a word that didn't sound strange, but when I woke up I couldn't remember it. I could guess what the familiar voice in the dream was asking: it wanted me to reach out my hand and grab the knocker and pull it toward me and then let it slip from my fingers. I knew that, and I'd done it before, and I could do it again. I'd hear the brass strike the wood, and wake up.

JULIA WAS decorating the Christmas tree at our house when my mother died. I remember the clinking ornaments. All of us got together over the Christmas holidays of 1985. We didn't know that mother would be leaving us, and we didn't know it would be our last gathering. I remember how Julia hovered around the green pine tree that Ilya had brought in (it was a tall tree that reached the ceiling) and how she took the colored ornaments from Mary. I remember her glowing skin (she was pregnant), and Mary, in a blue dress, barefoot on the carpet, leaning over a burlap sack that we called an "onion bag" (the brown one was a potato bag, the red one was an onion bag). I remember Liliane combing the fur of the European dog she'd received as a gift. And Najwa was in the dining room, buried in exams she'd put off correcting until the final hour. I remember the sound of the radio (the old wooden radio whose base had dug a permanent hole into the dresser). The volume was turned up, and Najwa was calling Liliane but Liliane couldn't hear her, and Julia was laughing as she wrestled with the branches of the tree.

I remember Ilya coming and going while Julia told him "You

can't smoke here" and the tiny dog made a sound like the meow-
ing of a cat. I remember my mother calling me from her room (my
father never came home before evening, and it was still midday). I
went into her room and saw that a glass of water had fallen over on
the nightstand. She said the glass was empty—or nearly empty—
as I picked it up and wiped off the water that had spilled with a
tissue. I sat down beside her on the bed. She held my hand, and it
was only then that I noticed she wasn't well.

"Are you tired?" I asked her.

"I'm going to die now."

I remember the noise from the radio, I remember the din of my
sisters outside. I remember the door slamming and someone talking loudly. Then the radio grew softer, and the voices died down.
My father came into the room.

I still don't understand how he knew she was asking for him—
he'd been at his office at the port.

I think a lot about the strange things that happen. While I was
studying at Sacred Hearts, I heard a story that resembled my own,
though I didn't know it at the time. There was a line of stores across
from the gate of the school. One store sold *Sahba* toys and candy
and jam (and for a while the owner put in a falafel fryer and started
selling us sandwiches as well). And there was a store beside it, I
can't remember what all they sold there, but it was the only place
in that area where we could find "Lion" chocolate bars. The owner
was a blind man who we'd often see playing the oud, and we sometimes tried to cheat him (by giving him a piece of paper instead of
a banknote, or by giving him a one-lira note and telling him it was
a fiver), but he'd just laugh and hit us playfully without getting upset. Past those two stores, there was a shop that sold both fish and
flowers. We'd head over there, not for the flowers and the fish, but
rather to look at the owner's daughters. The owner was originally

from Tripoli, from the Khodr family—I think he was a relative of Bishop George Khodr. Each of his daughters was more beautiful than the last, and they all resembled one another, even the youngest one, who wasn't actually their sister. The owner's name was Nadeem Khodr, and when he found the young girl he put an ad in the papers with his phone number on it, asking "anyone who knows anything about her" to contact him. Have you heard how he found her? During the Two-Year War, he was living in the town of Dbayeh, and was on his way back home to his wife and daughters when the refugee camp started burning. Gunfire sparked against the walls and sprayed the sidewalk as he struggled to cut through the smoke. He finally reached the building where he lived. As he went through the dark entryway, escaping the stray bullets and mortar shells and exploding glass, he stumbled on a basket. It was just like the basket we use for fruits and vegetables: the baby had been wrapped up and left in it. The man took her in and raised her as his own. We used to see her sitting in the store with her mother, in the middle of the tanks full of colorful fish, and we couldn't believe it: she looked like a younger version of her mother. She looked just like her sisters, as if she were one of them. I don't know if she knew or not. Did she know her family wasn't her own?

Years later, that story from my childhood came back to me, and I tried to remember what I thought—and what I felt—when I'd first heard it. I couldn't remember. All I could remember were the girls' beautiful faces and the brightly colored fish, the aquariums and the bouquets. Is her story like my own? The smallest of details is enough for the two to be completely different. Here, where I'm putting my finger—this is where the bullet entered. If it had been an inch lower, it would have pierced my heart. (I know a man who now lives in a village about twenty kilometers outside of Melbourne. His name's not important. He was Ilya's friend, but he left Lebanon in '87, and he's been in Australia ever since. He's married to an Australian woman and has kids, and he carves wooden masks in the simple style of the Aboriginals. He has exhibits of his work and people buy his carvings, and that's enough for him to live on. His wife used to punch train tickets, but now she's left her job and stays on the farm with him and raises the kids. They have some cattle, and also some fowl. When Ilya traveled to Australia a few years ago, he went and visited him on that farm in the country. I remember that man sitting on the roof of our house, after the Mountain War but before my mother died. I can't remember when exactly, but sometime between '83 and '85. I remember him taking a small cloth bag that looked like a glasses case out of the pocket of his military jacket. The bag had a leather cord. I remember him untying the cord while turning the bag over in his hands, as if there were something alive inside the bag: butterflies, for example, or bees, or cicadas, I don't know. That's how he was moving, that's how his fingers were moving. I remember the boy I used to be — how old was I? twelve? thirteen? — and I remember that boy turning around and looking at his big brother's friends, who had all fallen silent. He was opening the bag, and everyone's eyes were glued to it. He opened it and turned it over into his outstretched palm: I saw marbles, or what I thought were marbles. They looked like small strangely colored glass globes, and I couldn't figure out why a fighter would collect them. When one of them said they were all from Shatila, I didn't understand what he meant.)

Why am I telling you this story? The bag was full of human eyes. Why am I telling you about this? Because it's a part of me. When I studied Heraclitus in college, I was struck by this sentence: "A man's character is his fate." What did he mean? Isn't the opposite true as well? Doesn't fate make a man's character? All these coincidences that happen in the course of a life — don't they form who we are? But he meant something else. I think about these things, and as I think about them solace comes.

We went back to the house after the funeral. Clumps of dirt appeared on the stairs as we climbed up them: mud from the grave. My memory of the funeral is nothing but darkness. I was there, but I can't remember a single thing. All I remember is a hand pointing at a tall building in the distance: the family graveyard is near the demarcation line, and it isn't safe there when the snipers on the eastern and western sides of the city are exchanging fire. A lot of families stopped burying their dead there. They switched to Mar Mitr, even though that cemetery never used to have people from our denomination.

We buried my mother next to my little brother and went home. My sister Mary made a beeline for the kitchen and started heating up the food. She took a pot out of the fridge and put it on the flame. Then she filled a bucket with water from the faucet and put some cleaner in it (a white powder with red beads). She got out the mop and the broom and went out to the stairwell. I looked at her, and at the face of someone else standing by the stairs who was also looking at her. That's when I noticed there was no one in the house. Where had they disappeared to? They were all here a moment ago. My mother had died and the family had vanished.

I stood at the door to the house and watched Mary splatter soapy water (was that soapy water?) onto the stairs. The sound of water on the tiles. Mary was taking off her slippers (were those slippers?) and a thick foam flowed out in front of the broom. I looked over at the stairs that led to the roof and saw some muddy footprints. Who'd gone up there? My father? One of my sisters? I heard a voice behind me, in one of the rooms. Who'd closed the door to that room? Why was it closed? My mother had died and the family had vanished. I went down the stairs. "Be careful," Mary said. Was she afraid I'd slip on the soap? Or was she afraid I'd get the stairs dirty again? I stuck to the wall, going down two steps at a time, and didn't slip on the soap. I went out into the cold. I remember the stinging air, the clear blue sky, and the northerly wind blowing. . . . At the end of the street, near the old eucalyptus tree, I saw two kids playing catch with a ball. I stood and stared at them. I stared at the ball coming and going, coming and going, and felt an inhuman hand plunge down my throat, pass through my chest, grab hold of my guts, and pull them up between my teeth like a bag of yogurt. But that wasn't the worst moment. At night I lay stretched out on my back with my eyes open. I was covered in a wool blanket, and there was a quilt on top of the blanket, but my teeth still chattered. A horrific chill had taken hold of me. Now when I remember the first night after my mother died, I remember how cold I was. Even though—and this seems strange to me—the cold never bothered me back in those days.

I think I dozed off for a moment. I *did* doze off for a moment, because when I opened my eyes and looked at the sofa where Najwa had been sleeping, no one was there. A faint light was seeping in through the stained glass, the glass of the new door we'd installed between the living room and the corridor after Ilya had broken the old one. Night had fallen, and I pricked up my ears but didn't hear a sound. A car passed by outside the house. I got up to look for my father. I couldn't find him. I went to the room where Ilya slept. Ilya wasn't in his bed. Where had they gone? I saw a light under the door of the room that we still called "Julia's room," even though she was married by then and had left the house. I pushed open the door and saw Ilya, Mary, Liliane, and Najwa on the bed. I approached silently and sat down among them. I saw some of my mother's things on the pillow: the prayer beads; the watch with the silver dial and the leather band; and the thin gold chain with the oval pendant that contained two pictures (a picture of my father when he was a young man with long sideburns, and a picture of Maroun the deceased).

Years later, when I discovered I wasn't myself, I remembered that moment from the Christmas holidays in 1985: opening the door and seeing, beneath the lamp, Ilya and Mary and Liliane and Najwa sitting on the bed.

My mother died, and the distance between my father and the rest of us grew. He had already been distant before. Then my mother passed, and he grew more distant still. He didn't come to Mary's wedding. He blessed the wedding and told the groom, "You're my son now." But he said he was tired and couldn't handle a wedding. Mary was crestfallen, and for a while she didn't come visit us, but then she did: she kissed my father on his head, then took his hand and kissed his fingers. He pulled her to him and asked her how she was.

It was Najwa who said he was putting walls up around himself. She'd go up to the roof to sit with him, and he'd run away from her, he'd escape to his birds: he gave them some seeds, changed their water, cleaned their cages, and moved the cages. He was running away. His friends — from his days at the port, and before that, too — had stopped visiting him because of his mournful silence. They'd ask him questions, and he wouldn't answer. Then he'd get up and leave them alone with Liliane in the living room.

I only have hazy memories of the time between mother's funeral and Mary's wedding. During the same period, Najwa quit her job at Zahrat al-Ihsan and worked for a little while at the Three Moons School, then she quit that job as well. She was taking a lot of sedatives. One evening, while we were watching images on the news from the War of the Camps, which was raging in West Beirut, Najwa said some harsh words to Liliane (she wanted Liliane to change the channel, but Liliane didn't change it) and got up and hit the TV. She hit it several times, and it went dark, and then she pulled the cord out of the wall and threw it on the floor. She punched the door as she stormed out of the room. Liliane and I were left sitting in front of the silent television. I opened my mouth and said something. I don't know what I said, but I don't think my words were the cause of what happened next: Liliane turned toward me and told me to shut up and not get involved. Have I told you how her face changed in the blink of an eye, how she turned from an angel (Liliane had my mother's beauty) into a devil? My words didn't cause that.

After '85, the house began to close in on us. My mother was gone, and we all went our separate ways. The house began to feel cramped. If I saw my father's cigarette glowing on the balcony, I'd go up to the roof, where it was cold, and the night air bit my skin, but I'd still go up to there. If the balcony was empty, I'd go out there instead, because that meant my father was up on the roof. Back then, my father and I used to change locations as if we were taking turns on guard. Ilya didn't join us in the game. My mother's death drove him out of the house. The Mountain War was his first departure, but not his last. Weeks after my mother's funeral, he started squatting in a building in the Furn al-Shabbak district. He said he was renting it, but we knew his friends, and we knew that all of them were taking over apartments in Ayn al-Rumana and Sinn al-Fil and Furn al-Shabbak—the apartments of people who'd left the country.

They all left, but instead of the house getting bigger, it started feeling cramped. I remember Mary standing on the narrow kitchen balcony, waiting for her fiancé. The kitchen balcony overlooked the street, and she'd already be on the stairs before her fiancé even honked the horn of his Buick (the horn scared the birds). She'd leave in the early evening and come home after midnight. No one said anything to her, not even Julia. Times had changed — it was like my father was no longer in the house. "He's not eating anymore," Najwa said. My father *was* still eating, but he avoided sitting at the table. And it's true he was eating less. He ate standing over the sink, or he'd take his food to the balcony or up to the roof: the birds were his excuse. He wouldn't say anything. He punched more holes in his belt: his pants were becoming looser around his waist. He usually got dressed early in the morning and kept the same clothes on all day. He still hated pajamas, and he'd always put them on just before going to sleep — we'd only ever see him wearing pants and an unbuttoned sweater over a shirt. But all his elegance was gone. His clothes were too big for him now — it was like he was wearing someone else's clothes.

George Sader (our brother-in-law) was the one who helped Najwa move to France. You remember the '80s, how the dollar was doing, and how the lira crashed. Everyone's money became worthless, people saw their savings vanish, but our brother-in-law made quite the profit: his currency exchange was flourishing, and he was on cloud nine. He helped Najwa: he contacted some relatives and people he knew in Paris, and in a few days he'd found her some work. But before that happened, before Julia got involved and asked her husband to contact some people in Paris, Najwa got into a fight with Ilya.

I didn't know all the details. I knew Najwa was having an affair with a married man. I knew Ilya was unaware of it and then found out from one of his friends. Then he "lost his head." That was his expression, he was the one who used it afterward, while he was explaining what he'd done to Julia and Mary: he didn't hit her, no, but he swore at her and said some things she couldn't bear ("they're saying my sister's a whore, they're . . ."). He gave her a mouthful, and when she stood up to him, he pushed her (I wasn't there, but I can imagine the scene). And he threatened her too.

"You're not my father."

She didn't back down. He hit the walls and shattered the vase that had adorned the dining room table for as long as I could remember. Then he punched the door and left the house. Najwa said the only things hurt by his outburst were the canaries and his own knuckles — that's what she said, but I could hear her saliva as she swallowed it.

A few weeks later he came and kissed her head and apologized. I don't know what he whispered in her ear, but I saw him hug her while she tried to escape from his embrace. Then she let him apologize to her. I left the room and stayed in the kitchen till I heard Ilya calling me.

Najwa's departure was delayed a bit because of the paperwork: it took time to get the papers ready and gather the necessary signatures, and obtaining the visa took some time as well, but all of that was taken care of faster than I'd thought possible. While Najwa was packing her bags and telling me she didn't ever plan on coming back to "this unlucky country," I realized I was closer to her than to the rest of my family, and I'd never realized it until she was laying her open suitcases on the living room floor and on the sofas and folding and stacking her clothes. . . . I remember the reddish light of the setting sun (we had temporarily removed the sandbags from the windows to let the house breathe a bit), I remember that color flowing into the living room and flooding her luggage, and I remember how the light rose until it reached the picture.

She had booked a spot on a ship that sailed regularly from Jounieh to Cyprus. All of East Beirut traveled that way back then because the road to the Beirut Airport was blocked. The airport was in West Beirut, and it was easier to cross the sea to the Larnaca

Airport in Cyprus. I remember her closing the suitcases and ty-
ing small red ribbons around the handles so she'd recognize them
once she arrived in Paris. I remember her taking a teacup she
loved — a teacup with Chinese drawings on it — out from among
the dishes and trays in the cupboard, and how she took her time as
she wrapped the cup in an old newspaper. I remember music coming in through the window, and I remember the one suitcase that
remained open till the very last minute, and how the light of the
setting sun filled it. I didn't feel sad. I was happy for her.

Was I happy? My father, who was standing on the balcony in the
middle of the canaries, waved to her as she walked to Ilya's new
black Range Rover. The sky was overcast, but the sun came out for
a moment and I saw my father up above, among the birds spreading
their feathers, and he seemed to be smiling. Was he really smiling?
I told you memory can play tricks on us.

I remember us in the Range Rover, and I remember Najwa turning around for a moment, double-checking that all her bags were
there, and looking through the darkened glass at the ghost left
behind on the canaries' balcony. Najwa never saw my father again.
She didn't come to the funeral when he died.

Ilya's Range Rover took us to Jounieh on that overcast day. He
later gave that car to Liliane as a present when she got into the
Jesuit University. She studied there on a fellowship, and I studied
at the American University (AUB), also on a fellowship. When I
applied to AUB, I was expecting to be studying at the East Beirut
branch. I didn't know at the time that the war would end suddenly,
that the East Beirut branch would close, and that I'd find myself a
student in West Beirut. I submitted my application and took the
entrance exams. There were three exams. The first was called S.Q.,
and was a science and math exam. The second was called E.E., and
tested one's English. And the third was the "skills" exam, which

was for people who wanted to study engineering. I took those exams before the end of my senior year of high school. School was frequently disrupted back then. I told you that after the death of my mother, I felt like I was walking through fog—did I tell you that? When I think back to Mary's wedding, for example, it's all very hazy: people were dancing and I couldn't understand why. I remember the decorated cars in front of the church, the flowers (their smell was suffocating), the photographer, and how he stuck his video camera—and then his head—out of the car's open sunroof. I remember Ilya with his friends, a procession of Range Rovers, green and silver and black. And I remember young girls carrying trays of baklava and chocolate.... I remember the children in their shiny shoes and black neckties, and Mary in a dress that fanned out like a white cloud, that spread like the fog that trailed me from Sioufi to the church, and then to the strange house where Mary would be living from that day on, then back to Sioufi again. What was I feeling? I didn't feel anything. How did I feel on the sidewalk in Jounieh when the long ship started moving and the colored balloons rose to the sky?—and who sent them up? How did I feel when we got back home—just Liliane and father and I? And how did I feel when Liliane asked me if I had a girlfriend at school?

I swam through the fog for years. I was always wearing a black leather jacket back then, which Ilya had given to me on one of his short trips to the house during the battles on Mount Lebanon. When I first tried it on in front of the mirror by the stairs (there was an old closet near the stairs leading up to the roof, and there was a mirror on the closet door), I heard him laugh and say I'd lost weight while he was away. As the years passed, I put on some weight and began to fill in that black jacket. The leather cracked while I was swimming in the fog. At school we used lighters on our jackets to know which were real leather and which were fake.

I don't know how those years flew by: large parts of that period escaped my memory unseen, as if the years had fallen into that thick fog as I was walking forward, as I was trying to turn around to see where they'd landed, as I was trying to stay present. I lost them, and maybe there's nothing I could have done. Now, if you asked me which of my memories are real and which are false, it would bring up a lot of fear. I'd be afraid of not being able to tell them apart, afraid of losing myself between two people.

The clashes in the heart of East Beirut shut down the school on several occasions. Sometimes I felt I'd never make it to college, that I'd be stuck in that high school for all eternity. I didn't want to be stuck there, but at the same time I didn't know where to go. I wasn't Ilya. I used to watch Ilya buying and selling cars, then working for secret organizations, and then going back to cars again. I used to watch him and feel a terrifying impotence: I felt I was weak. Once he took me to see his place in Furn al-Shabbak. On the way there he bought some falafel from a store, and some roasted chicken from another store, and "something to drink" from a third store. At each stop, he'd grab his gun as he got out of the Dodge, and when he returned he'd throw the bags in the back seat and set his gun down on the floor of the car. Every time he got out of the car, he'd slip the gun under his belt. I thought we'd never make it to his place. He kept taking back roads, turning left and then right. . . . I asked him if he was lost. He laughed, smacked the steering wheel, and he said he loved spending time with me, that he missed me. He asked me why I didn't come and live with him. "But where's your place?" I replied, and he started laughing again. He asked me if I ever went to the movies, and if I had a girlfriend. . . .

"She seems interested." That's what Antoine Tannouri said to me in English when the dance was over.

He and I were getting ready for the E.E. exam together and trying to talk to each other in English as much as possible. At that party, everyone was speaking English and laughing. That was something unique to the parties in Achrafieh during the War of Elimination. After speaking in English, Antoine would laugh and adjust his glasses on his nose. I hadn't noticed she was interested until he said so. In general, I never noticed anyone, and never thought that she — or anyone else — could be interested in me: I didn't notice because I wasn't there — but where was I? I don't know. On our second dance, when the music was slow, she spoke into my ear. She dropped the English and told me she liked the way I walked: she always saw me on the street and she liked how I walked. No one had ever told me there was something special about the way I walked. I didn't know that.

I remember her blue *Mujer* sweater, and its soft fabric. After that, anytime I saw her dancing in that sweater I'd tell her I felt something moving in my heart. But I didn't tell her I was falling for her as she pulled me closer while we danced. She pressed me against her body, and I felt the beating of her heart, the solidity of her body. I felt no fear, and I thought it was the very first time I hadn't felt fear. But I *was* afraid. Was that fear?

Weeks later, when we were at the cinema, her hand in mine, I remembered Ilya laughing in the Dodge and smacking the wooden dashboard. The clashes were moving from one area of East Beirut to another, and we took advantage of each "period of ceasefire" to see a new movie.

I'd drive her car while she switched stations on the radio and the night spread over the sea. We'd talk or make out in the parking lot while we waited for the movie to start. Back at the car after the movie, we'd take our time leaving the lot. I remember a tree with many branches, and the thick shadows beneath it. I remember the cars' headlights.

What else should I tell you? We've all had those kinds of experiences. When Ilya gave me the key to his new apartment in Kaslik (he bought that one; he said he was trading fuel now) and I told her about it, she asked if I thought about my dead brother, if I thought about my brother who'd been kidnapped. I said I thought about him sometimes, but that I didn't remember him very well because I was so young when they kidnapped him.

She sat on the edge of the bed and said she was thirsty. I was as embarrassed as she was, or even more so. I went to the kitchen and opened the fridge, which was full of bottles of water and soda and vodka and juice. There were countless types of cheese on the top shelf, and beside the fridge, in a basket made of bamboo, there were bottles of wine.

I came back to the room and saw her dress on the chair. She was under the covers, laughing. I remember her short-sleeved blue silk top on the back of the chair. I remember the feeling in my chest: emptiness. As if my soul had left me. As I embraced her and then entered her, the emptiness receded, and I felt a fullness within me.

We fell in love, and my mind was running wild, making plans, and running wild some more when she told me (on the upper floor of a patisserie on Mono Street that's no longer there — she was eating ice cream and I was eating cake) that she couldn't see me anymore. She said we had to break up. She said her father had asked that of her. She said her father knew our family and respected our family, but that he thought we weren't right for one another. She said she couldn't go against his wishes.

After my father's operation, Ilya started visiting us every weekend. On one of those weekends, I found myself at Hilda's place, sitting across from her father, listening to him speak without knowing how I'd come to be there. Hilda had disappeared after the meal, and her pale and sickly mother disappeared too, leaving me alone with him. Even the maid had disappeared. I don't want to say that I hate him — all of this happened years ago, and it isn't important anymore. He spoke about my father and said he knew the sacrifices he'd made. And he spoke about my brother and said he knew he'd been injured on the mountain. He fell silent for a moment, then told me he knew a lot of things about our family — "You have no idea how much I know, my boy" — and that he really did respect our house, but he knew what was right and what was wrong better than his daughter, and better than myself. "She's not right for you, and you're not right for her." That was the gist of it, and the words hadn't bothered me, but that look: once again, I found myself subjected to that strange look. Why was he looking at me like that? I wanted to ask him: "Why are you giving me that look?" But I didn't.

Did I say his words didn't bother me? That happened a long time ago, years ago — it's easy to forget now. I saw Hilda in a dream after we broke up: she was walking on the edge of a mountain that was on the verge of collapsing. The place was similar to the Burj Hammoud landfill, and I could see piles of dirt sinking into the sea. The ground was sliding away beneath her as she called out. She was calling out to me (but wasn't saying "Maroun") as I ran toward her. Then the landfill disappeared, and so did the sea.

After the invasion of East Beirut, they arrested some of Ilya's friends from the old days, then they were released. Antoine Tannouri and I crossed the demarcation line while they were digging up the remaining barricades with bulldozers. The war was over, and we were going to explore West Beirut. I didn't find a ruined black city — no, I saw a city that looked like East Beirut. If you asked me what my first impressions from that trip were, I'd say three things: the dialect was different, there were a lot of run-down buildings, and the crowds were awful. We went into neighborhoods that frightened us: throngs and throngs of people.

We didn't stray from campus much during our first few weeks in college. Then we slowly started to venture out: we discovered the area between Bliss and Hamra, and we discovered the Manara corniche. I can still remember the carts with pistachios and cashews crossing Hamra Street at night, the bright yellow glare of the gas lanterns on the packages of nuts. Later, once the peace had become more stable, they made it illegal for those wooden carts to be out on the roads. I don't know why they made them illegal. They should have done the opposite, right? I used to buy nuts from them and go back to the dorm and call Antoine: he lived on the fourth floor, and I was above him on the fifth. I'd bring the nuts and he'd bring the beer.

I've told you before that something changed in me when I left the house in Achrafieh. To this day I don't know how it happened. Many years have passed since then, and what I do remember is unclear. When I try to tell you now about what happened back then, the memories merge with what I imagine to be memories. I don't know if you understand what I'm trying to say. I don't know if there's a way for me to express myself better. I remember, for example, standing on the fifth floor balcony one night, talking with my new neighbors: they were from all over, speaking different dialects, and some of them were in the business school, while others were studying engineering or chemistry, and so on. They had different majors and came from different places, and all of them had lived through the war the way I had, more or less. And now, like me, they'd entered a time of peace. When we talked, one of us would tell the others his stories — but cautiously, as if we were all moving through difficult terrain, as if we were checking the ground beneath our feet before advancing, before taking the next dangerous step forward. . . . It's possible the others didn't feel that way. But that's how I felt. I wasn't exactly on guard, but the whole time I could feel that I might (that

I *might*) be in danger. On the other hand, I felt safe. That was very odd to me: to feel safe among all those strangers who were living in identical rooms on the fifth floor of that building — it was strange to feel safe away from my father's house.

The disturbing dreams kept on coming. The face of the blonde woman I'd seen years earlier in the safe room refused to leave me. I didn't run away from her, quite the contrary: I loved how she showed up in my dreams. She seemed to be looking for me, and I started waiting for her to show up. Then I began to get nervous: who was she? Had I seen her before? Where? When?

Before the end of the first month, I'd become friends with a student in my department (mechanical engineering). His home wasn't far from the university — it was in the Verdun district, above Hamra, and he could walk there in ten minutes — but he lived in the dorm, even though his home was nearby. His room was above mine, on the sixth floor. He told me he preferred living away from his family: he felt free here, in the dorms. We'd walk around the campus, beneath the trees and the lanterns. Whenever the electricity went out (and back then it still went out a lot), cries rose up in the dorms, and darkness engulfed the campus: that would last a few brief moments, until the generator kicked in and the lights came on again. We could still see darkness outside the campus walls — I'm telling you about this because those brief moments had an effect on me: the second the electricity went out and the cries rose up in the dorms (they'd scream and laugh as they stood in the darkness in front of their rooms), I felt a limitless power gather around me. The power was on my side, it wasn't acting against me. I felt — this is what I'm trying to say, but I don't know if I'm getting the message across — I felt that windows I'd been unaware of were opening up inside me. I felt that things I didn't know, secret things, were on the verge of appearing.

Now I realize that was both memory and imagination—but how could I tell the two apart? I was reading Saint Augustine, thinking about the old days when the small buzzer went off in my room: I rushed down to the telephone room by the entrance to the building and picked up the phone, my heart beating faster than usual. I heard Ilya's voice. The book still in my hand (it wasn't mine, it belonged to one of my neighbors who read strange books, he told me about that one so I opened it . . . later on, I wound up reading it several times), I heard Ilya's voice coming from a distance, from behind the demarcation line, from East Beirut.

In the Rizq Hospital, while they were cutting my father's forehead open for the second time, Ilya told me we needed to prepare for the worst. I drank some water from a bottle and looked at the chairs across from me. The scene was repeating itself: we were sitting in the same waiting room as before, staring into the same emptiness. Even the gate that overlooked the trees was half-open, as it had been the last time. A feeling surprised me: the feeling of distance. It wasn't just my body that had moved away from home. My mind had also begun to move away. Ilya was saying something, but I wasn't paying attention—I was thinking about how it was midnight and that at this time I was usually standing on the fifth-floor balcony looking at the distant lights glistening on the hills, and at the lights of the fishing boats glistening on the open sea. I was thinking about how I always stood on the balcony at night—how I'd hear everyone scream the moment the electricity went out, how that strange force of joy emanated from the building—when Ilya told me what he hadn't been able to tell me the last time.

"There's something you should know."

ILYA TOLD me I wasn't myself: he said they found me on the demarcation line, bleeding from a wound in my chest. Later on, I'd hear the story I told you at the beginning (a car from West Beirut comes to an alleyway: something happens and gunfire rings out. Everyone in the car was killed except me. I was wounded in the chest, but I survived. I didn't want to die). I listened to the story as I looked at the white cloth wrapped around the head of the man who'd carried me, bleeding, away from the demarcation line, the man I always thought was my father. Who was he? The wrap hid half his face — half his face, the top of his head, and one of his ears. And it hid parts of his neck too. Who was he? What did his one remaining eye see in his final days? I lost myself in distant places. I don't know where I went after I found out. I remember walking on the campus streets and then leaving the paved road and walking among the trees: the grass and the soil and the dried leaves. The black stumps, a whitish color visible beneath the dead bark. Did I see anything? Who was I back then? Years later, I walked along that narrow path once more, among the trees that divided the upper part of campus from the lower. I saw green buds sprouting from the dead stumps that day, and flowers hidden in the grass, and I asked myself where he went, that person who walked this way years ago. Where did he go?

I want to tell you what happened to me, but I don't know how. Can you imagine how I felt when they told me, after all those years, that I wasn't myself? No one can express what's inside of them, they do the best they can, but in the end they can't actually express it. Now, when I try to find words to explain the feeling that came over me, I can only say this: "I was choking."

As I left them, I felt two massive hands around my neck. I kept walking, farther and farther away, I crossed the demarcation line, I passed by buildings, I crossed roads and whole districts, but the grip around my neck held firm. It was as if their words had clogged my throat. "You're my son," the man said. Another voice said, "You're my brother." And the third voice, what did it say? All those voices were choking me. I ran away.

But I didn't run away. I wanted some air. I wanted to breathe, but I couldn't find any air. Maybe I wanted something else entirely: maybe I wanted to choke, to choke completely. When I remember myself back then, I remember two people, someone split in two. I don't remember a single person.

The operation was a success. But the "success" only lasted four weeks. A third clot (the doctor said that was a possibility after the operation) killed the man who carried me from the demarcation line to his house in Achrafieh in 1976.

I went to his funeral. Ilya, who was crying, held my body between his arms. As I tell you this, I can see the stream of images in my mind. What is memory? Fields, yes, fields and palaces, caves and passageways. Right now I'm gathering up my memories and watching them flow, I'm plunging my hand into the stream and groping for one specific memory, as if looking for a polished stone that sleeps on the riverbed. That's what I'm doing when I speak to you: I'm extracting the memories from the back rooms, I'm taking untrodden paths to try to find myself.

The same place. It was raining. Ilya, with my sisters. The black colors, and the priest speaking words that were lost among the raindrops. I didn't go back to the house with them. I saw their faces from a distance, the rain was falling between us, and they were behind that glistening sheen. I left when they approached me. I went farther and farther away, I crossed the demarcation line, passing buildings and crossing roads and whole districts. I walked and walked.

When I sat on the bench beneath the trees of the campus, I felt cold. The rain was pouring down on me. Now, as I close my eyes, I can see myself there, and I don't see just one person. I see myself as two, as if I'd been split into two creatures, as if I weren't a man. After a while the rain stopped falling. I remember the orange light flooding the old building across from me, flooding the green plants that were creeping up the walls of the building, flooding the red bricks. The clouds subsided at sunset, and the cats came out and gathered on a patch of red light. But the rain was still falling inside my head. The man beneath the earth. Who was he? I sat on the bench under the trees. Who was I? I pressed my hands against my pants, I squeezed the water out of my clothes.

For a long time I couldn't breathe. Two people were struggling in my chest, I didn't know who they were, I didn't know how it would all end. I'm trying to tell you, but I know I can't.

I went to my classes and took notes from the lectures and went back to my room. I read what I'd written without understanding any of it, as if I'd forgotten the English language. Even the numbers, even the mathematical equations, even the symbols I knew so well, I no longer understood any of them. (Maroun used to know those things, but how could *I* know them? I? Who was that?)

That was the worst period of my life (*my* life? whose life?). I spent countless days hunched over my desk, copying out dark equations on a white page, a page that soon turned black: I wrote line after line, but the equations refused to reveal their secret. Antoine used to slide open the door to my room when he came back from the cafeteria: he stood over me and asked if I'd eaten. I'd turn around and look at him, also seeing the balcony and the white railing, the green cypress trees and the bricks of the math building, and I'd shake my head. Sometimes I wouldn't shake my head. Throughout that whole period of my life, I felt as if my back were broken. As if I couldn't stand up, as if they'd broken my spine. Antoine would leave and come back with a potato sandwich from the Universal shop by the campus. I'd eat part of the sandwich, but not all of it—I had trouble swallowing, and I'd tell him I'd finish it later, I'd tell him that I'd be up late and would finish it then. He'd leave and the door would slide back and hit the frame. He said he was worried: I'd lose my scholarship if I failed two courses.

Years later, when I was attending a training program in the Port of Hamburg, I met a woman named Christina. She'd come for the training, too, and we became friends. She told me she was going to work at the Oslo Airport after she graduated in a few months. We used to go to a bar near the old municipality building. We'd drink our beers, the foam overflowing, and eat fried potato sandwiches. Once, Christina told me a story, and as she was talking, I remembered the dorm room, and the potato sandwich (what was left of it) wrapped in paper on the desk, while the wind blew outside (when night advanced, the wind would blow and bend the tops of the cypresses and beat them against the balcony railing, and the rain was pouring as I stayed up late in the light of the desk lamp, which hovered above the dark equations. . . . It was cold, very cold. An electric heater with glowing red coils sent out a bit of warmth at my feet, and the tea kettle was whistling). Christina was talking about her father while I listened, feeling like I was back there, back in that room I'd left in Beirut. . . . I remembered the details of the room, but I couldn't remember the person sitting at the desk. I only remembered that his back was bent, that he had dark circles around his eyes, and that he was sprouting a beard—it had been days since he'd shaven. This is what Christina told me while we were smoking, after eating and drinking our fill, and before we went out into the rainy night: her father was from a village famous for making a specific kind of sausage. But he didn't work in that trade—her father raised fish and pickled them. And he had a hobby he loved: picking mushrooms in the Black Forest. He used to pick mushrooms in some rough terrain, and one time he fell between the rocks, he fell into a crevice and hit his head. When he opened his eyes, all he could see was darkness. Then he saw the stars in the sky. Before he saw the stars, he thought he was dead. He thought that was death. And then he realized he wasn't dead. He wanted to move, he tried to get up, but couldn't. He was caught between two rocks, stuck there, and he couldn't get himself out. He was covered in dew. The dew was cold and icy—that was the Black Forest, that was high ground. Do you know the Black Forest? After some effort, he managed to move, he managed to escape from the grip of the rocks. At that moment he noticed he couldn't remember who he was. He hadn't realized it the whole time he was struggling with the rocks to free his body, but once he'd managed to get out of the crevice and was standing on the ground among the trees, he realized he couldn't remember where he'd come from, he couldn't remember who he was, he didn't know his own name.

Christina fell silent and looked at a loud group of people who'd entered the bar. They were drunk and wearing summer clothes, even though it was cold. I asked her what happened to her father next.

She said he climbed a tree and looked for a light, just like people in the stories, and when he saw a light he walked toward it. That's how he reached the village. He went to the first house he could find and knocked on the door, and when an old woman with disheveled hair opened it (she was terrified, it was late) he asked her if she knew him, if she could tell him his name.

Christina's story stayed with me. I wished I'd heard that story earlier, back when I was hunched over the incomprehensible equations in my room on the fifth floor, feeling the darkness steal up to my eyes. I remember my roommate snoring while I covered myself in a blanket and went out to the wraparound balcony and walked around the fifth floor, around the dark rooms, once, twice, three times. I went down the stairs, my slippers dragging on the steps. I didn't take the elevator because it sometimes broke down. If it broke down in the middle of the night, after midnight, you had to wait a long time for someone to wake up. I went down to the entrance of the building, looked at the locked telephone room and at the black phone motionless beneath the light. I don't know why they'd left the light on. Then I went to the foyer and turned on the TV. On other occasions I kept on walking. I went out to the oval lawn, I went farther. I saw students up late studying in some of the classrooms, a single student in each room. The light was brighter here. White neon. I saw a tired face look up from a book and stare right at me. I saw a large cup of Nescafé beside the book. Did I see anything? Now, when I recall what happened — so I can tell you about it — I can see things I didn't see back then. Even though they were right in front of me.

If I'd heard Christina's story back then, would it have done me any good? Her father climbed a tree and looked for some light. He knocked on the first door and the old woman opened it. He asked her what his name was, and she told him: she knew him. But me — who knows me?

The small buzzer in my room went off and my roommate said: it's for you, not me. I left the room and walked the length of the wraparound balcony to the staircase, then went up to the sixth floor. I stood up there and looked out toward the sea. I didn't go down to the telephone room, and I didn't answer the call. I knew who it was.

I still don't know how I passed the exams. I didn't fail two courses, I didn't even fail one. Who was studying in my place while I looked at the symbols without grasping their meaning, without knowing what they were?

I told you not to judge me at the beginning of my story. Time passed, and when the buzzer sounded again, I went downstairs and answered the phone. Ilya said he'd come by the dorms twice and hadn't found me. I was surprised, because no one told me someone had come by. I told him I didn't know. He said he'd broken the phone trying to call. "Najwa's been calling you too, from Paris."

A few days later the buzzer went off again. I heard Najwa's voice coming from a distance, the connection kept cutting in and out. I heard some of the words, and some were lost en route. She asked me to come visit her during the vacation: "I want to see you, my brother, I want to sit and talk with you. Come to Paris." She said she'd book the flight and mail me the ticket.

Don't judge me. Antoine and I spent the vacation in the microfilm section of the university library looking through newspapers from '76 for a burned white car (burned or riddled with bullets, empty or full of corpses). We looked for a wrecked car in the area around al-Burj Square, and we found hundreds of cars: some were white, and some were other colors. We decided to look through the obituaries. We tried to learn something from the pictures of the dead, and from their names (countless pictures, countless names). We knocked on every door. Antoine tried to convince a judge who was a relative of his to look through the records of the domestic security services: the judge laughed and said all the records from the war — and especially the Two-Year War — had been burned. They'd been burned or lost or stolen or destroyed. The records from the motor vehicles registry had also been burned (that was Antoine's suggestion, to look for a white Mercedes or a white Opel). What do you do when you climb the tree and can't see any light?

Ilya helped me too. He's the one who remembered Evelyn Azar. He found her phone number in an old notebook, hidden inside a dresser drawer. He contacted her and arranged a meeting for me. When she opened the door of her house in the Ramil district, she was holding a handkerchief. She coughed and covered her mouth. She said the flu was merciless. I spent twenty or thirty minutes in her house, and we split our conversation between the flu and the period when she "took care of orphans at the beginning of the war." She said she found homes here and abroad for countless orphans, and she said she couldn't help me because she didn't know anything about me. She'd helped make arrangements for so many orphans — but they were numbers and names to her. And she asked me why I didn't check with the mayor.

Ilya told me — when I spoke with him — that the mayor he remembered from the time had died several years ago. But even if he hadn't died, what would he know?

Antoine suggested we put an ad in the paper. I felt drowsy (after the exams, my body collapsed: I was tired all the time, like I needed to sleep, but when I lay down on the bed I couldn't sleep. I only slept a little, sometimes the whole night would pass and I wouldn't sleep more than two hours), and replied: "What would we write in the ad?"

The way I walked changed. While I was walking on the streets that ran from Bliss to Hamra, I'd turn and see, reflected in the storefront windows, a person hunched over like an old man. There was a knot at the base of my spine in those days. Was that a memory or my imagination? That's how I remember myself back then. And my eyes were bloodshot.

When the pain in my head kept me from sleeping, I went to the university clinic. You know the clinic: it's near the dorm, buried in the shade of giant trees. The place was empty then, during the break between semesters. I remember how slowly I walked, how I stepped on the dried leaves in the passageway—I heard that distant sound (something dry cracking) without understanding it. What was there to understand? I remember the sour taste in my mouth, the acidity rising from my belly as I leaned against a tree. There was a metal plaque on the tree: the words "Origin: India" were engraved on it, and the tree's flesh had grown over the edges of the metal plaque. I placed my hand over the piece of steel, covering it. I still, to this day, visit that tree whenever I'm passing by.

The doctor asked me if I smoked or drank. He didn't get up when I entered his office. He lifted his head from his papers and motioned for me to sit down. His white robe was unbuttoned, and the whole time I was there he kept playing with the stethoscope around his neck, as if he were trying to fix it (or break it). From the beginning, he had an antagonistic look in his eyes, a look of utter contempt. He noticed I was silent, that I'd come in and sat down and forgotten to speak, and when I told him what was wrong, he said migraines were common both during the exams and after them, they were caused by the stress, when you get stressed your brain becomes fatigued and revolts. He didn't approach me, and he didn't touch me. I thought it was better like that—did I want him to touch me? Did I go there for that? He wrote me a prescription on the white stationary with blue lines, and he was breathing with difficulty (did he have asthma?). He handed it to me, and I looked at it and saw that special handwriting the doctors have, which only the pharmacists can decipher.

The pharmacist told me the medicine was excellent, much stronger than Panadol, but without any of the side effects. All of this is etched in my memory: the tree outside the clinic, the doctor's white robe, the scrawls on the paper with the blue lines, the container the pharmacist tossed onto the glass of the table that separated us. Why do I remember all those worthless details while my old name lies buried in oblivion? In bed, I used to struggle to remember my first name (sometimes with my eyes closed, and sometimes with them open). I struggled to remember who I was, and the more I struggled the more I forgot. There was a point when I even had trouble remembering the house in Achrafieh.

Then that night came: it was hot and I woke up panting, out of breath. I was drenched in sweat, and the smell of the smoke that clung to my fingers and pajamas and hair made me feel nauseous. As if it weren't my smell. As if it were the smell of someone else who'd come while I was sleeping and put on my body and my pajamas, chasing me away to hell. I was woken up by a headache, the likes of which I'd never known. The pain was focused on a single point above my right eye. I felt the blood surging in my brain, I felt it becoming heavy, I felt it crying out. My brain was full of blood. I held my head between my hands, I wanted to scream. My roommate was asleep. He wasn't snoring for once, but he was fast asleep and unaware of everything. I was in hell, and here he was sleeping. I was afraid the blood would start coming out of the pores around my ears (afraid? — fear wasn't even possible, that excruciating pain didn't leave room for anything, not even fear). I got up and went to the bathroom. I washed my face. I put my head under the cold faucet and let the water run over it. But the headache didn't recede: it grew sharper. My head was heavy, I was resting it in my hands, afraid I'd fall (I almost fell). I swallowed the medicine with a lot of water. I sat down at my desk and turned on the lamp. I heard my roommate mumble in his sleep, and saw some movement beneath the covers, but then it subsided. I opened and closed my eyes, trying to get rid of the pain, but it was useless. It felt like the blood surging in my skull was putting pressure on my eyes from within, as if it wanted to flow out of them—my right eye felt like it was about to pop out of its socket.

I couldn't even stay seated on the chair. I stretched out on the bed once more. I pushed away the pillow (it had become hard beneath my head, and my head couldn't take it anymore, which was becoming more and more sensitive, even my own touch caused it pain). My head sunk into the bed. Nothing like that had ever happened to me before. I raised my body once more and leaned my back against the wall. The small fridge that separated the two beds was giving off its familiar hum: I tried to focus on it. Maybe I could distract myself from my head that way. When I remember that night now—that night in hell—I wonder if my mind really was revolting, like the doctor had said. Had I worn myself out studying the law of gravity and the equations for electrical circuits and free falling bodies? Had I worn myself out studying how matter turned into energy (how light speed was reached)? Had I damaged my mind while I was sitting in the microfilm room, turning the roll by hand to look at the tiny black words on the yellow screen? I saw the words and the old black-and-white pictures, I saw Karantina and Tel al-Zaatar and Jisr al-Basha. I saw the roads, the piles of corpses on the roads, and the fighters trampling the corpses, making toasts as they drank champagne from overflowing bottles (there were some faces I thought I remembered—a fighter with a black beard, his big eyes looking at me with affection). I saw corpses lying on the ground. And I saw three young men with rifles hanging around their necks. One of them was pointing at the half-naked corpse of a woman on the road. Another one was carrying a guitar and had thrown a large shawl over his shoulders — no, not a shawl, I don't know what you call it, it's like what the Mexican peasants wear in American movies. Had I damaged my brain, looking at those faces smiling at the camera? Was there still water on the road (or was the picture blurry)? Had I damaged my brain while I looked at picture after picture, remembering my father — were those my memories, or were they Ilya's? — as he headed home, the strong smell of smoke and blood coming off his clothes?

I wanted to get rid of the pain. I wanted to scream. My head was in my hands, and it wasn't my head. It was as if some inhuman power had removed my head while I was sleeping and put this other head in its place. But it *was* my head. It was heavy, and the blood was boiling in my brain, and I felt like I was dying: "If this pain doesn't stop soon, I'm going to die." That's what I said to myself. The pain was so bad I couldn't breathe. I tried some breathing exercises (long inhales and long exhales). "My brain needs oxygen," I said. I tried, but I couldn't manage. I stretched out on my back and surrendered to the pain — surrendered? I don't know what I was thinking at the time. I stretched out on my back and said to myself, "Let it go, let the pain in my head go, let this pain be gone." I grabbed my penis with my hand and started pulling it from its base like I used to whenever I had a high fever when I was young. I pulled on it from the base, I put pressure on it with the palm of my hand, I tried to focus all of my body's energy there — maybe the pain would leave my head, maybe the pain would move around, maybe it would spread around my body and my head would feel a bit lighter. As I pressed down with my hand, I saw a red cloud pass through my brain, and with all the strength I had left I summoned some images to save me: I entered the dark palace of memory and summoned them. There were countless rooms, but I couldn't see them because the doors were closed. I kept calling them, I summoned Hilda and she appeared, her body white and naked: she came and slept beside me in my bed, and she put her hand on me. I'd asked for that, I'd asked for a hand to touch me. Was I real? Was I actually there? The red cloud spread across my eyes and blurred her face. Her face disappeared, I tried to remember it, but she was gone, as if she'd been buried there, while the torn plastic bags slid away, and the soil slid away, and the old cans slid away, and the slashed rubber tires slid away. . . . Everything was sliding into the sea, the whole dump was collapsing, and now garbage was floating on the surface of the water.

I called out to the people I knew, I called out to the living and the dead as I lay on my back, speechless, breathless, in that room on the fifth floor. I called out and no one came. Where had they gone? I pressed a hand to my head, and the pain got worse until I almost screamed. I pulled my hand away. I didn't know what was happening to me. It was as if my brain were splitting in two: Was there a tumor in my head? Was I dying of cancer, just like my father? (I said "my father." I was in hell and without noticing it I said "my father." I said the words and felt them, and I saw the man looking at me with his one remaining eye as I came home one evening, my face dark. He was sitting in the entryway, across from the door, and he raised his hand, and I raised mine. I didn't look at him and I didn't stop and I didn't talk to him: he raised his hand weakly, and I raised mine.)

I wanted to scream. The pain was unbearable. I know as well as you that no one can communicate their pain. Whoever tries to speak their pain keeps repeating the same words, over and over again, boring the listener. They wear themselves out in the attempt to communicate what's happened to them, what's afflicted them, and it bores the listener. I know. Pain's like that. It's indescribable.

Do you know how I fell asleep again? Do you know how it left me, that headache the likes of which I'd never experienced before? While I was moaning, I began saying, "Oh Lord, make this pain go away, O Lord, make it go . . ." Was I praying? Was I delirious? How high was my fever just then? It was a hot night. (Was it hot? My roommate had covered himself with a blanket and I didn't see him take off the blanket for the whole night.) Was my fever high? I don't think it was that high. So I wasn't delirious. What was it, then? I think I was praying as I called for the pain to leave my head. I think I was praying.

I've told you the details of that night because a few days later, while I was washing my hair under a cold shower, I felt something warm coming out of my ear. I touched my ear as I turned off the water, then got out of the shower and looked in the mirror: I was bleeding.

It was just a few drops. I dried myself off and got dressed and went to the clinic. My hair was still damp when the doctor took a look at me. (This was a different doctor, an older one. He was tall, and he hunched over when he walked: I still see him walking through the campus sometimes, I like to watch him from a distance.) He used some cotton and those small plastic sticks. He inserted the cotton into my right ear, then into my left. He asked if I was taking any medication, and I told him the name. He nodded his head and said something. Was he speaking in Latin? He wrote me a prescription pad for a different medication, but said that getting rest was more important. "Go for a walk on the corniche every day." He lifted his eyes from the prescription before stamping it and said, "Walking's the best medicine for headaches. Drink some water too, that'll really help. Look at this beautiful campus. You're in the dorms, right? Go for walks at night under the trees instead of sitting in front of the TV. Don't think too much, and you'll get better."

Was I thinking too much? I wasn't thinking. I didn't have the

capacity. All I wanted was to remember. That's what I'd been trying to do the whole time. Didn't I tell you that I'd split in two,
didn't I tell you I'd become two creatures in a single body? There
were two of me studying for those exams (one of them was studying while the other tried to remember a life he'd lost when they
opened fire on the white car). There were two of me poring over
the newspapers in the fetid microfilm room (one was looking at the
titles, keeping an eye out for keywords, and the other was trying
to remember an old name that had been lost among thousands).

Years later, during a company business trip to Dubai, I met up
with a friend from my days on campus, someone I used to see sitting in front of Antoine's room, on the wraparound balcony: he was
one of Antoine's neighbors and was always sitting at the same spot,
drinking tea, or Nescafé with milk, and reading Superman comics.
He was always reading those comics — it was as if he never went to
class. If he disappeared from the chair it was because he'd gone to
the movies or to the cafeteria or he was playing checkers in the West
Hall and watching the girls. We sat in the lobby of the Jumeirah Hotel in Dubai, and he told me he was a civil engineer (I never saw
him on the engineering part of campus while I was there, nor do I
remember ever seeing him on the steps of the engineering school).
I learned he'd moved to Colorado, where his siblings lived, after two
years at AUB (that's true: after my sophomore year, I no longer saw
him in front of Antoine's room). All of his siblings worked in America and had families there. But he didn't like the country. He started
laughing as he put his hand on my shoulder in the hotel lobby. "Let's
have dinner," he said, "I want to tell you something."

Over dinner — we sat on the top floor, he ordered prawns with
rice and I ordered roasted lamb — he told me this was the best
job in the world. "If you want to know what mankind's capable
of, you've got to be in our line of work," (he said it like that, even

though I'm not a civil engineer). He told me he'd been in Hong Kong two months earlier, and asked me if I'd ever visited there. He said the subway system had multiple levels, and whenever it got too crowded they'd dig down another level into the earth. And it was the same with the bridges. Whenever the traffic got too bad, they'd go up another level by building a new bridge on top of the old one. And that wasn't all: the freeways that surround the island and allow you to circle Hong Kong while you're in your car, drinking tea and listening to jazz, all those roads are built on the sea, on water, they're built using land that's been brought in. Just like here, he said.

He asked about the university and about the dean (I was teaching the first-year mechanical engineering course, ME 201, at the time). I told him it was the same, it never changed. He laughed and said his father says that too. His father graduated from AUB in 1961, also in engineering: "He still goes to campus and sits there with his friends — can you believe it?"

He asked about Antoine. I gave him his e-mail address.

He asked about Rhonda (a woman Antoine once dated). He laughed when he saw the indifferent expression on my face. And I thought of Ilya while he was laughing. We'd finished our food before he finally told me the story (he'd been waiting for the noise to die down and the crowd to get smaller — people he knew kept coming by to say hello): His brother, who worked in Austin, had come back to Beirut a few years earlier to help with the expansion of the airport. The company he works for over there — in Austin — was a partner in the project. His job was to supervise the transportation of the support beams (the piles) into the sea. Those beams were important for the new runway. He wasn't the only supervisor. He worked in conjunction with the Lebanese engineering firm Dar al-Handasah. He wasn't exactly the "supervisor." You could say he was a consultant, or one of the consultants. First he got the steel beams ready at the Dar al-Handasah headquarters by the airport, then he transported them in trucks to the Ouzai coast. It was summer, and the heat was intense. The bulldozer was clearing some space on the beach when its blade dug up some corpses. He saw the corpses, but at first he didn't know what he was looking at. Then the truth hit him. Just a few days earlier, he'd been telling his wife on the phone—his wife worked in Austin, she had a pediatric clinic there—he'd been telling her that Lebanon was changing, that everything he loved about the place was still there, but the stuff he hated was beginning to change. His wife didn't like the subject, and she'd gotten annoyed. She wasn't fond of Lebanon, and didn't believe she'd fully left it behind. "We should come on one of our short vacations and you'll see how much it's changed," he said. "Let's just come for one vacation, just like that, without any plans, so you can see for yourself." That was before he saw the bulldozer blade slice into the corpses and lift them into the air, before he saw the sand and bright pieces of clothing fall from the corpses. The driver turned off the engine (an oily cloud filled the air) and got down from the bulldozer, muttering "In the name of God" and "God protect us." He stood there, looking at the body parts, then turned around and looked at the engineer who'd come from America. "What did he say to him? I don't remember. But this is what I do know: My brother's in America now. And I don't think he's coming back to Lebanon ever again."

I stopped taking the first medication, the one the pharmacist claimed wouldn't have any side effects (I took out the little pamphlet and read about eleven different side effects. I counted them—they weren't numbered on the pamphlet, but I counted them: there were eleven of them). I didn't bleed out my ears after that. (One of Ilya's friends was playing cards on the roof of our house after the Mountain War with his right ear and his right eye wrapped in bandages. He hadn't been hit, but during one of the battles he'd fired a large number of RPG-7 rockets. His launcher had cracked and he knew it would explode on his shoulder if he fired it again. The flames had burned some bushes behind him and exposed his position. He found new cover and grabbed a launcher from a wounded friend. He fired that launcher till his ear started bleeding. He kept firing even after that. But he stopped when blood began streaming out of his right eye. His eye couldn't stand the pressure.)

By the time the new semester started, my roommate had stopped sleeping in the room. He came every week or two to turn the room upside down looking for something or another, and then left. Sometimes I'd get back from my classes and see him with some friends from outside the university standing in front of our door — out on the wraparound balcony — jostling one another and shouting and laughing. They played children's games together, which always surprised me. They'd form a circle with one of them in the middle, and then they'd hit the man in the middle on the back of his neck while he turned around and jumped and tried to protect his neck with his hands. The man in the middle's task was to figure out who had last hit him: if he figured out who it was, he'd get to leave the center. They'd open up the circle whenever I approached, and I'd pass through and enter the room and throw my notebook on the bed before continuing to the bathroom. They always asked me to join them, and I never knew how to reply.

A few weeks later I discovered that I suddenly had a single room, that I'd been left alone there. My roommate had left the university without telling me. One of my neighbors from the other end of the fifth floor told me when I ran into him in the elevator. He said my roommate had gone back to his family in Jordan, and wouldn't be returning. I waited another week before getting a cardboard box and putting all his clothes and books in it. I put the box under his bed and forgot about it. Did I forget? Whenever the Bangladeshi workers came to clean the room (sweeping and mopping), they complained about the box and started laughing. They put it up on the chair or on the table and kept on laughing. At that time in my life, people seemed to be smiling and laughing everywhere I looked. I even started running into the friends of my former roommate, who weren't students from the university (one of them told me the name of the university where he was studying), whenever I crossed Bliss Street or rue Jeanne d'Arc, and they'd say hi and talk to me as if I were one of their closest friends. They'd laugh and slap me on the shoulder with their strong hands while I remembered how they used to stand in a circle in front of my room, in their brightly colored shirts (which were clean and ironed), a strong smell of perfume coming off of them. When I think back to them now and talk about them, I miss them — can you believe it? One of them always wore a yellow shirt and had a pair of those "Texas" boots that were so popular back then. He used to smack his hand against the boots. When he saw me taking some eggs out of the fridge to boil them, he'd laugh and say: "Nothing's more important than eggs." He'd crane his neck through the doorway as he stood outside with his friends and say that expression of his and laugh, and I'd laugh too.

Did I laugh? I painted different expressions on my face. It's enough to depict the emotion, right? If you frown, the people around you think you're sad. And if you smile, they think you're happy. I used to paint expressions on my face. Now, when I talk about them and remember how they'd open up the circle and ask me to join in, I know that they too are part of my story (though I don't know their names).

In the evening, I used to leave campus with Antoine or another one of my friends and go for a walk on the corniche. Sometimes I'd go by myself. I started preferring walks by myself — I could walk at the speed I wanted then, and if I wasn't in the mood to talk, I wouldn't be forced to talk. Back then, crowds used to throng the corniche at night: carts selling corn and fava beans and chestnuts and pistachios dotted the sidewalks, and people were celebrating every night of the week. There were lovers sitting on the guardrails, and cars drove by with their doors wide open and video cameras on their roofs. I got in the habit of walking in the other direction, away from those crowds. I'd walk from the lighthouse near the university toward the military baths. That stretch of the corniche was less crowded. I didn't walk toward Ain al-Mreisseh.

I was following the doctor's orders. I walked and listened to the sea. The waves crashed against the wall and their spray rose up above the guardrails. I felt the moisture on the side of my face. I changed my course slightly, moving away from the rails and the spray, and kept walking, until, at a certain point on the path, I saw the beam from the lighthouse up above, spinning and cutting through the black sky. The cars passed by while I turned around and went back the way I'd come. I went out and walked on the corniche every night. Sometimes I'd see young women from the university jogging in their sports clothes, with headphones on their ears and small Walkmen in their hands. One of them looked at me once as we passed each other. She was in one of my classes, and I only noticed her after she'd greeted me.

I mention that woman merely to say this: I was there, and others saw my face and recognized me, remembered me. I was there, but I wasn't fully paying attention. That's all.

Was it the walking that helped me, or the passing of time? The semester went on and I went to all my lectures (attendance is mandatory in engineering) and wrote everything down in my notebooks.

One time I was in the big hall (its name was ELH) and the professor was writing something on the board that was related to the Second Law of Thermodynamics, and I noticed I wasn't copying down what he'd written. I wasn't writing down the symbols and equations, I wasn't even writing in English. I looked down at the page and felt nervous (afraid?). The page was covered in ink. A single word in Arabic had been written over and over again in tiny handwriting (as if it weren't my own), from the top of the page to the bottom: *ismi* ("my name").

I got better in spite of this—I could feel myself getting better: I started seeing colors again, smells slowly came back to me, and sounds began reaching my ears. I slept at night. And I had dreams while I slept, some I'd remember, and some I'd forget. I'd see faces I knew and faces that were blurry, as if they were slipping away beyond the fog. The faces that slipped away disturbed me. But still I got better.

Final exams came round again, and this time they were easy. My friends said they were harder, but they were easier to me. I didn't run into any difficulties in my sophomore year. I discovered I loved studying: I loved opening up a book and spending my night in an ordered world, a world with laws. Once you've grasped those laws, you can accomplish anything you want: you won't run into any problems then. I loved studying, and I loved reading. I still enjoyed literature as well as science. I studied Sophocles and the Greek tragedies (an elective course) in my junior year. I remember the professor of that course. In the very first class, he asked us who believed in fate and who didn't, and had us raise our hands while he counted them. That was quite an unusual thing to do: he seemed extremely interested in the subject.

Engineering was a four-year program. I took a year off from my studies after I graduated. A lot happened in the four years I was in college. I grew close to some friends, and grew apart from others. I discovered certain things, and forgot others. To cover my costs, I worked a bit in the library, in the lab, and in the telephone room. I visited places, and came back from places. So many things happen in life, things are constantly entering into you and filling up drawers in the storeroom of your memory. Did I change while I was in college? One changes all the time. And at the same time one doesn't change at all. Are tragic events the only ones that cause change? Perhaps those moments cause us to pay closer attention to what's important. Maybe not in the evil hour itself, but with the passing of time, when we remember them, we pay attention to those things.

A lot happened in those four years. A building fell in the heart of the university. It was during the night: we heard the explosion and went out to the balcony and discovered the clock tower was gone. The tower fell, and the telephone room was turned into an international call center. I haven't forgotten those nights after College Hall and its clock tower were bombed, as I sat in that office lit by a yellow lamp, taking calls from Jordan, the Gulf, Europe, Australia, and America. . . . I even took a call from the Comoro Islands. A man called and asked for his son (room 419), and as I pressed the button I asked myself: where are the Comoro Islands?

Ilya used to come and visit me, and we'd sit and drink Nescafé and talk, or we'd go outside and walk around the campus, or go to the cafeteria, or go out and eat something in one of the nearby restaurants. He loved the hamburgers at the Universal sandwich shop. We'd sit there and talk and eat while I thought back to the very first time he took me out to buy a sandwich like that. (I was sick with measles — I told you about that — and once I'd recovered he took me out and bought me a hamburger and a bottle of Pepsi. It was the first time I'd ever tasted a burger. The mayonnaise dripped onto my fingers. And the sesame seeds from the bun fell onto my shirt—he brushed them off with his hand.)

On one of his visits he told me he'd decided to get married. On the next visit, he said he'd made up his mind: he was never getting married. He laughed as he said this, and I laughed too. On another visit he told me about his new project: he'd rented a place in Achrafieh not far from the house and was getting it ready—he was going to open a sandwich and shawarma shop.

I used to see my sisters from time to time. When I noticed one of Julia's children looking at me with the same big eyes as the boy whose picture was hanging in the living room (a black ribbon in its corner), when I noticed his gaze and saw him turn toward me so that I'd play with him, I asked myself: How does time pass?

After graduation, I rented a house on Makhoul Street, near the university, with three friends. I worked for a while in the maintenance department of the American University Hospital, and the administration sent me on a ninety-day training trip to Johns Hopkins in America. As we were making our first rounds of the place, one of the engineers there told us: "It's not healthy for hospital machines to break down." On another one of our rounds, I met a doctor of Lebanese descent, and we talked. He knew I'd graduated from AUB, and he told me he came to America with his family during the Two-Year War, but that when the Two-Year War ended they didn't do what everyone else did: they didn't go back to Beirut, they stayed in America. He invited me to his home in Baltimore. His wife was Italian and made pizza or spaghetti every day, and he still loved Turkish food and peppered rice because he was used to it. His daughter was twenty years old and loved Japanese food—"And she's right," he said he and his wife agreed with their daughter on that point. The two of them always went out to Japanese restaurants, but he preferred—on his days off—to stay at home and cook beans or cabbage stew. He said he even made stuffed vegetables, and that his daughter had a particular fondness for his stuffed zucchini and grape leaves. Before I headed back to Beirut, he asked if I'd consider moving to Baltimore if there was a job opening. I said I didn't know. "Is there an opening right now?" "Maybe," he replied. He fell silent for a moment, then said it was possible. I don't know if it was possible or not, but I went back to the American University Hospital and finished the year there, and when the year was over I got a fellowship and continued my studies at AUB. I'd gotten used to the university, and found myself liking it. In the apartment we rented on Makhoul Street, where we lived for three years, we used to laugh at one another because we were all engineering graduates and yet none of us knew how to fix the kitchen sink. The apartment was in an old building, there was mold on the kitchen walls, and the light bulbs blew out all the time: we changed the bulbs each week, and they'd blow out again—the wiring was old. We didn't change the wires. At that age, you can put a lot of things off till the future.

Sometimes I'd see my mother in my dreams. I'd see my first mother, and I'd see my second one. I'd see the mother who died crying and holding my hand while I sat by her side on the bed. I'd see her face as she wiped off the icon of the Virgin Mary with some oil: she always turned around when she saw me come in with my backpack, my face all sweaty, and she'd smile and ask how my day at school was, if I'd eaten my sandwich, and what I learned in class. I remember the boy I was, I remember him skipping around the bed and taking out his books and spreading them on the carpet. He'd open the social studies book and show her the pictures. He'd say, "We learned some arithmetic today," and then ramble on while she listened. I saw him dart off like an arrow when someone called him from the kitchen, and I saw him come back with an apple or a cookie in his hand. In the dream I saw myself in the house in Achrafieh, and sometimes I saw my college friends there with me.

I saw my other mother too: the mother whose belly I came out of and who I've always thought died protecting me and my siblings from the bullets that sprayed the car. I saw my siblings too. Or rather, I saw the faces of children I thought were my siblings. I saw the blond hair and face of the woman I'd seen while I was half-asleep in the Sioufi safe room. These were visions — I wasn't actually remembering the scene in the safe room. I was dozing among the sleeping bodies, with rockets and machine guns firing outside, and she came and sparked a lighter to look for me. Was she looking for me? I thought she'd gone off with my siblings, gone somewhere far away, leaving me all alone to open the door and jump out of the car. They'd been firing and I hadn't heard it, I was asleep. When I opened my eyes, when the warm red liquid poured out of me, I stretched out my hand, pushed the door open (did I stretch out my hand? did I pull at the handle?) and got out of the car. I can picture the men in their raincoats, I can picture the white car beneath the rain, I can picture the glass shattering. I saw my mother in the dream, I saw holes in the collar of her shirt. A warm smell drifted in and I knew it was hers. What was she saying? What was she telling me? What did she want me to do? I saw her face — I think I saw it, the features came back to me after I woke up, but time has passed since then, and now the features have become hazy — but I didn't see my father's face. For some reason I could never see it. I didn't see his face, but I heard his voice in my dreams. He's the one who picked me up and told me to pull on the knocker on the green door and then let go of it. That's how you knock on the door. That's how the people in the house can hear us. They'll hear us and come and open the door for us — that's how we enter the house. (Whose house? Our house? The house of some of our relatives? Where was it?) I heard my father's voice without seeing his face, but I could see the features of an old house, and I think it was our own: the house I lived in until that day came and they sprayed us with bullets on the demarcation line.

I remember some details, like the wood-burning stove — you don't find those stoves on the coast, right? They're for cold climates, for the mountains. I could see the stove, the carved iron handle of the oven's small door. They told me to be careful when I opened the oven. My father did. I heard his voice, I smelled tobacco and sweat. That was his smell. I saw lemon peels roasting on the stove, their aroma filling the room. I heard his voice: "Don't leave the kitchen door open." Who was he talking to? The kitchen was warm, but the hallway was cold. I saw a window, I saw snow falling outside. I saw a trellis with grapevines climbing up the sides. I saw snow covering the branches, covering the ground, covering the water tank behind the trellis.

Some dreams repeat themselves, and some recede like the sea, never to be seen again. The years have gone by, and now I have fewer dreams. A couple years ago, I saw myself walking on a dirt road that ran through fields of fruit trees, and my father was walking in front of me. I saw him from behind, and I saw his hands, and the hair on the back of his hands, and from time to time he'd reach out and pick a leaf from one of the trees. I was waiting for him to turn around, waiting to see his face. I wanted to see that face. The sun was bright, shining on the leaves. I saw grasshoppers jumping in the sun-dried grass and a lizard basking on a rock. At a certain moment, I noticed my father had stopped and turned around: he was looking at me, he was staring straight at me while I looked around at the scenery, and he was smiling. I knew he was smiling. I lifted my gaze and looked at his face and knew he was smiling, but I didn't see his face. In other dreams he calls me by my name and asks me for something: I say something — I don't know what —

and start walking toward him. . . . But it seems like there's distance between us, like I have to cross that distance to get to him. At the halfway point, before I've reached him, I always wake up.

I'm telling you about these dreams not because they mean something, but because you asked. At one point it occurred to me to write the dreams down in a notebook. I thought that if I gathered all my dreams in one place and started to read them I might be able to put together whole scenes of my life from before '76. I didn't do it. I tried once. I wrote down a dream. But when I read it I discovered I hadn't written anything. I'd written some words, but they didn't recreate the dream for me. I don't know how to write. Writing's hard. When I wrote down that dream, I got lost in the details and couldn't figure out how to return to the scene I wanted to describe. The whole scene was lost in the details, and I couldn't find my dream in them. I didn't try again after that. Maybe I'd have more luck if I tried now. But I have fewer dreams these days. And when I do have dreams, they have nothing to do with my childhood: the years have gone by, and memory's palace has grown. New memories have formed on top of the old ones, and one floor buries another. My dreams have changed.

I love my work now: I love teaching, and I love the time I spend at the firm. Most of my work is directive, and our projects are split between Lebanon and the Gulf. At one point we wanted to expand (the others wanted that, not me—I generally prefer teaching to being at the firm). But we have a reasonable number of projects now, and we didn't expand. Sometimes I travel to Europe for work, and sometimes I travel on vacation. I've often thought about building a house somewhere in the country. With the passing of time, I've discovered I love nature. I love trees and I love gardening.

I've been living here for many years now. From the window (this window right here) I watch the sea at night. I watch the fishing boats, I watch the lights sailing away—I can't actually see the boats, but I can see their lights. I think I've spent many years of my life looking at those lights. There were times when they used to disappear, when night fell and the lights couldn't be seen. That would last a little while, but then a night would come when I'd see the lights again.

From that window over there, I look at the trees on the campus. I love those trees. They're old, and they were all brought in from distant places. They're still standing after all this time: they stay green the whole year round, and the birds build nests in them. In certain seasons, some of those trees are covered with red flowers that fill the air whenever the wind blows—you wouldn't believe how bright those flowers are.

I'm not young anymore. I'm close to forty now, and I can feel the years I've lived. The following date is inscribed in my passport and on my ID: September 29, 1971. But to this day I don't know the date of my birth. I don't feel like I'm thirty-seven, and I don't feel like I'm forty: I feel older than that. I don't consider myself depressed, but that doesn't stop the weight of the years from bearing down on me. Most of my friends are older than I am: I have two close friends here, at the university, and I have some friends outside the university, but most of them are older than me. That's strange, isn't it? Antoine once wrote that my sense of time has something to do with not having married yet. I asked him (we write e-mails to each other) if he got younger when he married. He replied with a smiley face. Maybe he's right.

I haven't gotten married, but I feel at peace. There were periods when I found it difficult to be alone. Now I've gotten used to it. I almost got engaged a few years ago, but then I didn't. When I tell you this now, I remember—I don't know why—a symposium at the university before I graduated. One of the associations for the kidnapped and the deceased in the Civil War had organized a symposium and were handing lists out to the people present: they were lists of the names of those who'd been lost in the war and whose corpses hadn't been found. No one knew, or no one could confirm, what had happened to them. I read those names, columns of names arranged like multiplication tables, and asked myself: Where's *my* name? Is my name here somewhere and I don't know it? And my mother? My father? My siblings? Are their names here too? But what if my father's still alive? Or my mother? Or my siblings? How could I be so sure my family died in the car? Maybe they're still alive. Maybe I'd gone out with a different family, with some relatives, with an aunt or an uncle — how do I know? Maybe my family's still waiting for me, this very moment.

I don't think about those things anymore, and I usually don't talk about them. I don't like talking. It's been a long time since I've liked talking. I'd rather look out this window. I *do* like teaching, that's true, but when you're teaching you don't feel like you're talking. I don't quite know how to say it, but words aren't the same as numbers and symbols and laws and equations: when I'm explaining mechanical laws, I don't feel like I'm talking. I feel like I'm silent. Silent and yet communicating with others. Silent and yet teaching others, guiding them. Silence: it's good. But I've talked to you. That's true as well.

I can tell what you're thinking from the way you're looking at me. But really, I'm not depressed. I'll tell you something: years ago, it occurred to me to celebrate my birthday. I knew the date, September 29, was an arbitrary one, but I told myself it was my birthday and I was going to celebrate. I'd never celebrated my birthday before, and I don't know why I thought about it just then, but that's what happened. My favorite patisserie was nearby, and I got dressed and headed over there.

It was closed. The weather was hot, humid, and there was a lot of traffic on the street. But I didn't turn around and go back. I remembered another patisserie I sometimes went to, farther away, but not too far. So I kept on walking. I said to myself: "If that one's closed too, I'll go back home."

It wasn't closed. I pushed open the door and went inside. The air was cool, and smelled sweet. I relaxed the moment I entered. The place was empty, no one was at any of the tables, and a woman (dressed in white) was sitting behind the glass counter with the cakes—a young woman, sixteen or seventeen years old, younger than my students. She smiled and asked what size I wanted (I'd ordered my favorite kind but hadn't specified how big a piece), then she pointed at two different sizes, medium and large. I ordered a large and sat down at a table by the window. The place was peaceful, and the sounds outside were soft, as if a great distance lay between me and the street. I looked at the cars and thought of distant things, and when I felt her lean over and put the plate on the table, I turned. She smiled at me, and I said thank you.

She said something to me, though I'm not sure what exactly. She might have been telling me to enjoy the piece of cake—I can't recall her words, but I remember her voice. She was pleasant, a pleasant young woman, and she set the piece down in front of me: the fork and the knife, and the plate with the large piece of chocolate cream cake in the middle of it. Then she went back to her spot behind the counter. That was all. But a pleasant feeling came over me.

I sat there, enjoying the calm—a strange calm that spread through me as I looked at the piece of cake on the plate and then turned and looked outside. Cars were going by. A man carrying a bag was walking on the sidewalk. Another man was pushing a stroller with a baby in it. A woman carefully got out of a car, almost falling over because of her high heels. A car horn went off: it was loud, but seemed soft and low to my ears. The window separated me from the street, and through it I saw people going back to their homes, and lights coming on outside: in the shops and in the homes.

I cut the piece in two. I ate the first half, then set down the fork and looked outside. Images, memories — so many of them — came and went as I sat there like that, though I didn't close my eyes. The place was calm. No one came in and no one went out the whole time. I could sense the young woman behind the counter, and I could hear soft music. But I wasn't thinking about her. I was there and I wasn't. I was somewhere else.

I picked up the fork and began eating the second half of the piece. It was the most delicious cake I'd ever had. I ate the whole piece and gathered up the crumbs on the fork and ate them too. I ate the whole piece, and felt happy.